"The only thing I'm lusting after tonight is food.

"Nothing else," Aaron added. He revved the engine and Kate slid quickly into the car, her face flaming with embarrassment and a tiny measure of annoyance.

Did he have to make it sound quite so ridiculous, as though no man in his right mind would ever want her? Gently seething, she stared silently straight ahead, refusing to turn her head and look at him.

"Don't sulk, Kate. It doesn't suit you."

"I am not sulking," she said sharply. "I never sulk."

"No? Well, I'd say you're giving a good imitation of it now. What exactly is bothering you the most—the thought of spending the night under my roof, or the fact that I'm more interested in my dinner right now than your charms?"

Jennifer Taylor, Liverpool-born, still lives in Lancashire, though now in beautiful countryside with her husband and young son and daughter. She is a chartered librarian and worked for the Liverpool City Libraries for many years. She has always written and has cupboards full of unfinished manuscripts to prove it. When she decided to try romance writing, Jennifer found it far more challenging and enjoyable than her other efforts. She manages to fit her writing into her busy schedule of working, running the house and caring for the children. Her books contain a strong element of humor, as she feels laughter is important to a loving relationship.

Books by Jennifer Taylor

HARLEQUIN PRESENTS
1326—A MAGICAL TOUCH
1349—TENDER PURSUIT

LOVESPELL
Jennifer Taylor

Harlequin Books

TORONTO • NEW YORK • LONDON
AMSTERDAM • PARIS • SYDNEY • HAMBURG
STOCKHOLM • ATHENS • TOKYO • MILAN

Original hardcover edition published in 1990
by Mills & Boon Limited

ISBN 0-373-03142-4

Harlequin Romance first edition August 1991

LOVESPELL

CHAPTER ONE

HE WAS there again, sitting at the same table, looking oddly out of place in his fine wool suit and silk shirt. Picking up a cloth, Kate wiped it over the counter to mop up the sticky mess of spilled beans and ketchup, her eyes lingering on the dark-haired man seated by the window.

It was the third time she'd seen him in here this week, yet why did he come? Everything about him screamed wealth and power; from the look of him he could afford to frequent the very best restaurants in town. So why did he choose to drink tea in this little back-street café?

'How about another cuppa over here, then, love? We haven't got all day, you know.'

The rough request drew her abruptly out of her reverie. With a sigh, Kate turned away, dropping the soiled cloth into a bowl before picking up the heavy pot to pour another cup of the dark brew which passed for tea. Setting the cup on to a clean saucer, she walked round the counter and across the room to where three men were sitting at a table littered with dirty dishes and overflowing ashtrays.

'Here you are.'

She bent down, pushing the debris aside to make space for the cup, feeling the men watching her, their eyes running up and down the slender length of her body. Colour flared in her face and she quickly straightened and turned to go.

'What's the hurry, darling? Surely you've got a few minutes to spare for good customers like us.'

The man who'd called for the tea caught her round the waist, pulling her roughly towards him, and Kate gasped in surprise. She twisted round, trying to break free from his hold, but his hands just tightened painfully round her slim waist. With a sudden jerk, he pulled her down on to his knee, his face mocking as he saw the annoyance in her huge green eyes.

'Let me go!' she demanded hotly, straining against him, using all her strength to force a few inches of space between their bodies, but he only laughed and pulled her back.

'Now that's not very friendly, is it, love? All I'm after is a few minutes of your company. Not much to ask, now, is it?'

The other two men at the table laughed as though he had said something brilliantly funny and Kate felt her annoyance flare into a red-hot anger. How dared he treat her like this, manhandle her in this fashion? Raising her hand, she caught him a stinging blow across his cheek, watching with a flicker of satisfaction in her eyes as his head snapped back on his thick neck. That would show him!

'Why, you little——!'

His face contorted in rage and in that instant Kate knew that he was going to retaliate and hit her back. She cried out, struggling wildly to free herself and avoid the blow.

'That's enough! Let her go...now!'

The sharp order was so unexpected that everyone stopped as though turned to stone. Suddenly Kate came to her senses and wrenched herself free, moving several yards away from the table and the three men. She looked round, wondering who had issued that terse command, and somehow wasn't surprised to find that it had been the dark-haired man sitting by the window. His whole bearing was one of such authority and power that issuing orders was obviously second nature to him.

He looked up at her, his face part shadowed from where he sat with his back to the window, yet she had the strangest feeling that there was genuine concern in his eyes as he studied her.

'Are you all right?'

Kate nodded, swallowing down the unexpected lump which rose in her throat as she heard the unmistakable evidence of that concern in his deep voice. It had been ages since anyone had been concerned about her, especially someone like this man.

'Now look here, mate. Just who do you think you are butting in like that? We were only having a bit of fun.'

The man who had grabbed Kate stood up, aggression in every line of his heavy-set body as he advanced across the room.

'Fun, was it? Perhaps for you, but I don't remember the lady laughing. I think you owe her an apology, *mate*, don't you?'

There was an edge of steel in the deep voice now, a sharpness which made Kate shiver when she heard it. She glanced at the man, watching while he sipped his tea, his eyes never leaving his opponent's face, and she had the sudden craziest feeling that he was enjoying the confrontation—but why? Why should a man who dressed like that and spoke like that enjoy tangling in such a game? Although he was broad-shouldered, his body lean and tough-looking, he would be no match for the thickset man who must outweigh him by several stones. Yet, still, she had the feeling that he was quite deliberately courting trouble.

'Apology! If there's any apologising to be done round here, it's you who will be doing it, d'you hear? You!'

Kate's assailant glowered down at the man by the window and she felt her stomach lurch in sudden fear on his behalf. She had to do something to defuse the situation and quickly, before he really got himself hurt.

'Please,' she said, her voice breaking the tense, expectant silence which filled the café. 'Please, won't you just forget about it, both of you? I'll bring everyone another cup of tea on the house. There's really no need to let this all get out of hand, now, is there?'

'Forget it, darling. It's too late for that. Let's just see if your knight in armour here is as good with his hands as he is with his mouth.'

Bending down, he caught hold of the lapels of the man's jacket and hauled him to his feet so fast that the table toppled over. There was the sound of crockery shattering, a blur of movement, and Kate closed her eyes, terrified to watch what would happen next. However, when she opened them again she had to stifle a gasp of sheer amazement as she took in the scene.

Her assailant was lying on the floor, a dazed expression on his face, while the dark-haired man was calmly smoothing his jacket down. He glanced up, smiling as he caught sight of Kate's stunned expression, his dark eyes holding a hint of satisfaction.

'Not very flattering to find you didn't think I stood much of a chance against him, is it?'

'I...I...' Kate cast round for something to say, something equal to the occasion, but frankly could come up with absolutely nothing. If she'd been setting odds then she would never have given this elegant stranger even the poorest ones against the ruffian now lying on the floor! She glanced round the room, studying the bemused faces of the other customers who seemed as stunned by the outcome of this mismatch as she, then smiled, a smile which lent an unexpected beauty to her face.

'Thank you,' she said simply. 'Thank you very much, Mr...'

'Blake,' he answered, crossing the room to stand just inches from her. 'Aaron Blake.'

He held his hand out and Kate slid her fingers into his, feeling the cool, slightly abrasive touch of his flesh against hers.

'Thank you, Mr Blake,' she repeated quietly, her green eyes level as they met the dark ones which were watching her with a strange, disturbing intensity in their depths. 'I really do appreciate what you just did for me.'

'Don't mention it. It was my pleasure,' he said, glancing down at his bruised, scraped knuckles with a wry little grimace. 'I've been itching for a chance to do that for the past half-hour.'

'What on earth do you mean?'

Startled, Kate stared up at him, feeling the way his fingers tightened round hers for the briefest moment before he let her hand go.

'Just that I'd got tired of hearing the way those men spoke to you.' He laughed, a thread of irony in the sound. 'Lord knows I never thought I'd come here and want to defend you. That was the last thing on my mind!'

Abruptly, he swung round and, pausing only long enough to snatch up the overcoat draped across a chair, walked from the room without a backward glance.

For a long minute Kate stared after him in utter confusion, wondering what he had meant by that strange little comment. It was crazy, but it had almost sounded as if he had come here to see her—but of course that couldn't be right . . . could it?

Kate had no time to dwell on the puzzle, however. Even working at top speed, she barely had time to restore the café to order before Tony Manetti, the owner, came back from his lunch break. She shot a swift glance round the room, hurriedly double-checking that everything was back in place, relieved that the three men had left shortly after Aaron Blake. There was no way she wanted Tony to find out what had happened today; it would only give him even more ammunition to fire at her, and he had quite enough of that, thank you!

For the past couple of weeks, ever since she'd spurned his advances, Tony had found every opportunity he could to take her to task. Now, from the look of his alcohol-flushed face, he would need little provocation to start off again. She would be well advised to make no mention of the incident and keep out of his way.

She hurried behind the counter and busied herself stacking clean crockery on the shelves, ignoring his hard-eyed glare. There was little doubt in her mind that things would have to come to a head soon, but if she could just ward off any confrontation for a while longer then she could buy herself a bit more breathing space to make fresh plans. She had been in this job nearly five months now, and, though the wages were low and the hours were long, she didn't want to lose it just yet. Along with the job came a tiny bedsit over the café, so if she lost the job she would lose that too: a doubly crippling blow. By dint of careful budgeting she had managed to save a few pounds, but a few more weeks would help her get back on her feet. No— she intended to hang on to this job just as long as she could, or at least for as long as she was prepared to put up with Tony's carping!

The rest of the day passed quickly enough. The café was busy and Kate was hard pushed to keep up with the serving and clearing the tables. Tony stayed in the back all afternoon, not offering to help even once, but she was glad. The further away from her he was, the better she liked it. There was just something about the way he looked at her, the way his hot eyes ran greedily over her slender body, which made her skin crawl. If Tony Manetti fell off the edge of the world one day then she wouldn't miss him!

It was nearer seven than six before she finally got away, and she climbed wearily up the steep staircase to her room, feeling her legs throbbing with tiredness. Her working day was supposedly from eight in the morning until six at night, but she couldn't remember when she'd last finished on time. There was always some job or other to be done before Tony would let her leave. Kate knew he was doing it deliberately to rile her, but she refused to be pushed into an argument. She needed this job, needed the money it brought in and the independence it offered, so she held on to her temper while inside she cursed the man with a fluency which once would have surprised her.

At the top of the stairs she unlocked the door to her room and walked wearily inside, leaning back against the flaking wooden panels while she caught her breath. She looked round, her eyes lingering on the colourful posters and cushions she'd bought to brighten the place up, yet nothing could disguise its basic shabbiness. Unbidden a picture of where she used to live came flowing back like an image from a dream, dim and slightly unreal. Was it really only a year since she'd lived in that smart flat, since she'd walked on thick carpet instead of cracked lino? Was it only a year since she'd slept between fine sheets in a soft bed instead of on a lumpy, pull-out sofa? It must be, yet it was a year which felt longer than a lifetime.

Now all that was gone, wiped out, erased like chalk from a board. That flat and the girl she had been, who had taken those luxuries for granted, belonged to the past. This was her life now and she had learned to accept it, but just sometimes she couldn't help but remember those days before she had met Jonathan Knight, and he had destroyed her life completely.

Suddenly frightened of where such thoughts could lead to, Kate moved away from the door and crossed the room to fill the kettle and make herself a meal. Working with food all day in the café usually meant that she had little appetite when she returned to the flat, but she always made herself eat something, even if it was only a sandwich. She had always been slim, her delicate bones holding only the lightest covering of flesh, but recently, with the constant hard work in the café, that slimness was verging on thinness. So far she'd been lucky, she'd avoided any kind of illness, but with the winter approaching she would have to be careful. She couldn't afford to skip meals; she had to keep her strength up because there was little doubt in her mind that Tony would soon find a replacement for her if she had to take time off. It had taken her months to find this job, and though it wasn't much it was a start, giving her a much-valued independence.

Her sister, Chrissie, and her brother-in-law, Jack, had done more than enough for her over this past year. She couldn't burden them again, not with their baby due to make its appearance in the next few months. Jack had offered many times to find her a better job in one of his hotels, but each time Kate had refused the offers. She had to learn to stand on her own two feet and make a new life for herself, no matter how hard it might be, and although she knew just how badly Jack felt about what his brother, Jonathan, had done to her, working for him wasn't the answer to any of it. Jack had no need to feel guilty, no need to take the responsibility for what his brother had done on to *his* shoulders, but it was so typical of him that he should want to do so. How could two men, brought up by the same parents and in the same family environment, turn out so differently? Kate didn't know, couldn't understand how one brother could have such high moral principles while the other had none; it was a complete mystery to her.

Sighing to herself over the vagaries of life, Kate cracked a couple of eggs into a bowl and made herself an omelette. When it was ready she tipped it on to a plate and carried it over to the table. One of the customers had left an evening paper behind in the café and she opened it up, skimming though the pages as she ate the omelette. She flicked a page over and suddenly a small, grainy photograph caught her attention. Setting the knife and fork aside, she smoothed the page out, wondering why the man in the photograph looked vaguely familiar. It was a poor picture, rather dark and indistinct, yet she had the feeling that she knew him from somewhere. Quickly her eyes skimmed down to the caption and she felt a start of surprise run through her as she read the name: Aaron Blake. It was the man from the café, yet why was there a photograph of him in the paper? Was he someone important?

Filled with curiosity, Kate read the brief paragraph then sat back in her chair, the omelette completely forgotten. The text had been short, just a few lines stating that top financier, Aaron Blake, head of Blake International, was in the area looking into the possibility of investing money in the dock reclamation scheme which it was hoped would bring cargo shipping back to the city. So far he had refused to be drawn on his decision, but hopes were high that he would agree.

So it seemed her gallant champion was indeed someone important as she'd suspected, but reading the confirmation of the fact only made his visits to the café seem even stranger than ever. Fair enough, she could quite see that he might call in once if he was in the area visiting the docks, but why had he returned again and again? The café was clean and the food wholesome, and Tony had a steady band of regular customers who used it each day, but Aaron Blake most definitely wasn't in that category. So why had he come back? There had to be something behind those visits . . . but what? Was it anything to do with that strange remark he had passed . . . was it anything to do with her?

The questions haunted her all night, drifting in and out of her mind, but when she finally did manage to fall asleep in the early hours of the morning she was still no closer to knowing the answers.

CHAPTER TWO

TONY was late . . . yet again!

Shivering slightly in the thin sharp wind blowing up from the river, Kate jiggled the key into the lock and opened the café door. She hurried inside, cursing softly as she made her way through to the back and switched on the lights before filling the metal boiler with water for the endless cups of tea she would pour throughout the day.

The café was situated close to a large hospital, and breakfast time was usually one of their busiest periods when one shift of nursing staff took over from another. How very typical that Tony should be late so that she would have to cope with it all by herself. It was the third or fourth time in the past few weeks and she was beginning to wonder if he was doing it deliberately just to annoy her. Frankly, she wouldn't put it past him.

Sighing to herself, Kate started on the breakfasts and had the bacon sizzling and the first orders served before Tony finally strolled in. He hung up his jacket and smiled at her, his dark eyes holding little warmth, just a malicious mischief which warned Kate she was in for trouble.

'So, it appears our little Kate has found herself a nice, rich protector, then, does it?'

'I don't know what you're talking about, Tony,' she said shortly. 'And frankly I don't think I want to know. There are people out there waiting to be served, so wouldn't you be better off dealing with them than making up silly riddles?'

She turned away, stripping off the grease-spattered apron before reaching for the blue-checked overall hanging behind the door. She knew what he was alluding to all right, his tone of voice had made it quite clear, but there was no way she was going to be drawn into playing any of his silly little games.

'Oh, don't play the innocent with me, Kate. I've heard all about what happened yesterday when I was out, about how that man sprang to your defence. Aaron Blake, wasn't it? Now I wonder why a man like that would risk getting himself hurt unless he thought there was something in it for him, eh!'

'I don't know what you mean,' she snapped, her face flaming at the undisguised innuendo in his voice.

'Come on, sweetheart, why play games? What's the problem? If you can pull a rich guy like that then why not? Just remember, though, that it was in Tony's café that your luck changed for the better . . . and be suitably grateful.' He stepped forward, sliding his arms round her waist to pull her against him. 'Don't forget now, Katie, that if it weren't for me giving you this job then you might be out on the street selling your wares to a cheaper buyer than Mr Aaron Blake. So why not show me how truly grateful you are?'

Catching hold of the back of her head, he forced her face closer to his, his fleshy lips parting in anticipation of the kiss he meant to take, but with a mighty effort Kate wrenched herself free. She rounded on him, her face filled with disgust, her green eyes spitting fury. She might be willing to put up with a few tasteless comments to keep the peace, but she wasn't prepared to put up with this!

'You keep your hands off me, Tony Manetti, do you hear me? Keep them off! Otherwise I might just have to go to your wife and tell her what you've been up to.'

It was her ace, the best card she'd been hiding up her sleeve for weeks now in case something like this happened, and Kate was glad that she'd played it as his flushed face paled. He stepped towards her, his hands outstretched beseechingly, but she stepped smartly back a pace, holding the overall in front of her like a shield.

'Now there's no need to be like that about it, Kate. I meant no harm. I only——'

'I know exactly what you meant, Tony, but now we understand each other clearly, don't we? You stay away from me and I won't be forced to tell tales about you.'

Without another word she pulled on the overall and hurried through into the café, feeling her whole body shaking with anger. She would have given anything to walk right out of the café and leave Tony in the lurch, but she wouldn't—not yet at least. She still needed the job for the moment, and the flat, but if he tried it again then to hell with it all. She wasn't prepared to take that sort of treatment from anyone! Still, maybe there wouldn't be a next time. The threat

of going to his fiery little wife had had a very damp-
ening effect on his ardour!

The busy breakfast-time session was followed by an
hour or so of peace which made the time drag. Kate
busied herself tidying the shelves under the long
counter and cleaning the small tables till they sparkled,
doing anything to stay out of the kitchen. Tony hadn't
spoken a single word to her since their run-in. He was
maintaining a brooding silence which Kate found a
trifle alarming. What was he plotting? What sort of
revenge for her impudence in threatening him? She
didn't know, but she had the uncomfortable feeling
it would be something unpleasant.

It was becoming increasingly apparent that she
would have to find another job soon, but what? With
the number of people out of work, which employer
would opt for someone like her, a woman who had
been at the centre of a major drug-smuggling trial?
She might have been found innocent of the charge of
bringing drugs into the country, might have been given
a total and unconditional discharge, but the mud still
stuck, and her name would still be linked with the
case for some time to come.

Only once had she lied about what had happened—
lied by omission really. She had filled in an appli-
cation form for a job as a counter assistant in a big
city-centre store, carefully omitting the fact that she
had lost all those months spent in custody from her
work record. She had been called for an interview and
had been fortunate enough to form an instant rapport
with the personnel officer. She had left the interview
feeling that she stood a very good chance of getting

the job. When the letter of rejection had come she had been devastated, so much so that she had taken the unprecedented step of phoning the store and speaking to the woman who had interviewed her. Even now, months later, colour still flooded Kate's cheeks as she remembered the coldness in the woman's voice, the curtness of her formerly charming manner as she'd briefly explained that there was no way the company could consider employing someone who had been exposed to so much unsavoury publicity. It wasn't the sort of image a respectable firm wished to foster.

Kate had felt sick to her stomach for days after that, but it had been a lesson she had never forgotten. There was no way she could ever truly escape from what had happened, no way it wouldn't have as much bearing on her future as it had already had on her past. There would always be someone, somewhere, who would recognise her and remember.

The bell on the café door tinkled sharply and, with a tiny sigh of regret for all she'd lost, Kate straightened. She glanced towards the door and felt every cell in her body start to tingle in sudden awareness.

Aaron Blake stood just inside the doorway, shaking raindrops off a dark trilby hat. He looked up, smiling faintly as he saw the stunned expression on her face.

'Good morning.'

'Er....' For a whole long second Kate struggled to find an answer to that simplest of greetings, feeling her face flaming as she saw the amusement glinting in his eyes. Despite what she'd thought last night when she'd read that article in the paper and wondered about his reasons for visiting the café, she had half expected never to see him again, but she'd been wrong. He was here now, and if she didn't manage to gather her addled wits about her pretty fast and speak he would think she was completely crazy!

Hurriedly she pinned a smile to her lips. 'Good morning, Mr Blake. I never expected to see you in here again after what happened yesterday.'

'It would take more than a lout like that to stop me, Kate. A whole lot more!'

There it was again, that touch of steel in his deep voice. Kate studied him thoughtfully for a moment, realising that behind the elegant façade lay a man who could handle any sort of trouble *and* anyone who caused it! As she watched, he shrugged out of his dark trenchcoat and tossed it carelessly over the back of a chair before sitting down at his usual table, and suddenly Kate remembered what she was employed at the café for. She picked up her pad and walked over to where he sat, adopting a formally polite manner to hide the confusion she felt at his sudden appearance.

'What can I get you?'

'Just tea, thank you.'

With a nod of acknowledgement she turned to go, stopping abruptly as he caught her arm, his long fingers cool and firm against her flesh.

'You look tired, Kate. Didn't you sleep well with worrying about what happened yesterday, or is there something else troubling you?'

There was a faint edge to his voice now, a strange hardness in the glance he ran over her pale face and the shadows under her eyes. Kate glanced down, studying the lean strength of the fingers encircling her arm, wondering what had caused it, wondering also how to explain that it had been his visits, and the reasons for them, which had given her such a restless night—nothing else!

'I——'

'Kate! Where the hell are you, girl? Come and get these sandwiches instead of skulking in——'

Tony pushed his way through the kitchen door and came to a halt as he spotted Kate and Aaron Blake. His eyes slid to her arm and Kate could almost hear his nasty lurid mind ticking over with a hundred unsavoury thoughts. She pulled away abruptly and hurried back to the counter, keeping her face averted from his mocking gaze.

'Come back for more, has he? Play your cards right, girl, and you'll soon have him hooked. He should be good for a pound or two, if nothing else.'

He didn't bother to lower his voice and Kate felt herself go hot with embarrassment and fury as she realised that Aaron Blake must have heard every word. Picking up the pot, she poured the tea, then set the cup on to the saucer with a sharp little clatter, hearing Tony's mocking laughter following her every step of the way as she carried it across to the table. She set it down, sickness welling into the pit of her stomach as she wondered what Aaron Blake must think of her now.

'Why do you put up with it?'

Blake's voice was low, for her ears alone, and Kate glanced at him, puzzled by the question.

'I don't know what you mean.'

'Him,' he answered coldly, his face hard as he looked across the room to where Tony was standing, elbows propped on the counter. 'Your so-called boss. Why do you put up with him speaking to you like that? Why don't you just tell him what to do with his job?'

There was open curiosity in his eyes now and Kate reacted blindly to it. There was no way she wanted this man to find out about her past; no way she wanted to see the scorn and distaste he must surely feel if he found out about the trial. She'd already seen that reaction before from other people: the surprise, the embarrassment, the sudden lowering of eyes unable to meet hers. She didn't want to see that sort of reaction from him. In some strange way it would hurt her more than any she'd experienced yet.

'Jobs aren't that easy to find round here, so I can't afford to be too touchy. But how about you? What brings you into the café?' She shot an assessing look at his expensive clothing, her face faintly mocking as she met his eyes. 'I doubt if this is the sort of place you usually frequent, Mr Blake!'

He laughed in wry appreciation of the small barb. 'No, you're quite right, it most definitely isn't my usual sort of haunt. Oh, years ago I must admit I spent a lot of time hanging round places like this, filling in empty hours, but those days are long since past.'

'I can imagine. I read an article about you in the *Echo* last night and quite frankly I can't imagine what brings a busy and important man into a place like this. We are truly honoured!'

'Even the busiest person needs to stop off for a cup of tea sometimes and this place was very handy.'

'Once maybe, but what made you come back time and again?'

His answer was more or less what she'd expected him to say, yet it still didn't truly explain his visits, or this feeling she had that there was something more behind them. Suddenly, Kate knew it was vitally important that he should explain why.

There was a moment's silence and she had the feeling that he was weighing up his answer with extreme care.

'Perhaps I just couldn't resist your tea, Kate,' he said finally with a dry little laugh.

Kate felt disappointment flare inside her as she realised that he wasn't prepared to say anything else. Still, in all honesty what had she expected him to say? That he had found *her*, not her tea irresistible? Surely that was reading far more into a chance remark than had ever been intended.

Kate laughed aloud at her own foolishness. 'Well, that's a good enough reason, I suppose. Now I'd better get back to work before Tony starts complaining again. Enjoy your tea. If what you say is true then it is obviously the stuff that connoisseurs dream of!'

With a last smile at him she hurried through to the kitchen to collect the sandwiches, almost dropping the heavily loaded tray in her eagerness to get away before Tony could take another shot at her. But she might have known he wouldn't let her escape that easily.

He followed her into the kitchen, leaning back against the door to block her exit, his arms folded across his flabby chest.

'What's the hurry, sweetheart? Frightened your Mr Blake might leave before you get back? I don't think you need worry about that. I've seen the way he looks at you. Can't take his eyes off you, in fact. Maybe I can find a few more like him for you...for a price, of course.'

He had to be joking! Unable to believe that she had heard him correctly, Kate stared dumbly back at him for a long minute, but there wasn't even the faintest trace of laughter on his face. He'd meant it, every single word, and the fury which had been simmering below the surface for the past few weeks rose up and erupted like molten lava.

'How dare you?' she snapped, her voice shaking with anger and disgust. 'How dare you suggest such a thing, that I'd be willing to sell myself? You have a filthy, loathsome mind, Tony Manetti, do you hear me? Now get out of my way, and never...*never* suggest such a thing again!'

She pushed past him, manoeuvring the heavy tray with difficulty through the doorway, aware of the unnatural silence in the café. It was obvious that the customers must have heard every single word and Kate wished that the ground would open up and swallow her. Face set into rigid lines of control, she unloaded the sandwiches, keeping her eyes averted from the table by the window. What must Aaron Blake be thinking? Would he believe that Tony's insinuations were right, that she made a habit of picking up men in the café?

The desire to know was so great that she couldn't resist looking at him, and she felt her breath catch at the expression on his face. Aaron Blake looked ready to kill someone, but whom . . . her or Tony? That was the question, a question she didn't have the right to ask. This man was nothing to her; he was a stranger who had come to her aid once, so why should she feel torn by the desire to know what he was thinking?

As she watched, he drained the last of his tea and stood up, tension in every line of his body as he shrugged on his coat. He picked up his hat then glanced across the room at her, his eyes glittering with some sort of emotion she couldn't quite read.

'I think it would be better if I left, don't you?' he said harshly. 'I seem to be causing you a lot of trouble and I didn't mean for that to happen.'

'But you will come again?'

The question rushed from her lips before she could stop it and his expression softened slightly.

'Yes, Kate. I shall come again.'

Reaching into his pocket, he dropped a handful of coins on to the counter, the clatter sounding unnaturally loud in the silence which had fallen over the room. Kate swallowed hard, knowing she couldn't let him leave thinking the worst of her like this.

'About what Tony said, it's not true, none of it. I . . . I just wanted you to know that.'

He looked at her, his eyes level and very dark as they searched her face, and Kate had the strangest feeling that he was trying to see deep inside her—but why? What was he looking for? What sort of answers to what sort of questions? She wished she knew.

'I know it's not true, Kate,' he said quietly, holding her gaze. 'One only has to look at you to realise that you are not that sort of a woman.'

There was a strange note in his deep voice, a touch of . . . what . . . reluctance? A feeling that he had made the admission almost against his better judgement? Kate puzzled over it as she watched him leave the café, but she could find no clue to what had caused it. Instead of learning more about the man, each time she saw him he became more of an enigma.

Lost in thought, she loaded the tray and carried the dirty dishes into the kitchen, sliding them into the hot, soapy water, barely aware of what she was doing. The soft sound of applause made her swing round and her face tightened as she saw Tony lounging against the open door. She turned back to the sink, scrubbing the cups and plates with unnecessary vigour as she tried to ignore him.

'Well played, Kate. A nice touch, that.'

'I don't know what you mean.'

She emptied the bowl, then ran clean water to rinse the crockery, splashing the front of her overall in her haste to be done with the job. She didn't want to listen to Tony, didn't want to hear any more of his disgusting comments. She'd had her fill for one day, thank you!

'Oh, come on, don't give me that. You must have spent hours perfecting just the right little note in your voice. "But you will come again?"' He gave a breathy imitation of her voice which made her cringe. Had she really sounded like that, both pleading and hopeful? She hoped not, but she had the uncomfortable feeling that she might just have done. She *had* wanted Aaron Blake to say he would come again so much.

'Anyway, I wouldn't worry if I were you, Kate. He'll be back all right, you can bet on it. But when he does you'd better make certain that you've got the next part of your act ready, and that you really understand what he's after.'

'What he's after... what do you mean?'

He grinned at her, his small dark eyes gleaming with malicious pleasure. 'Face it, love, he's hardly coming here to offer you marriage, now, is he? You're something new to a man like Blake. He's probably sick of all the society women he goes round with and you are something different, a fresh taste for his jaded palate. He probably feels that getting involved with a little waitress would make an amusing change, and you want to cash in on it while you can. Take him for every penny you can get, in fact.'

The words slid over her like iced water, chilling her to the bone as she faced the fact that Tony could be right. After all, why should a man like Aaron Blake bother with her unless it was for a new diversion, a way to kill a few hours? Tears pricked at the back of her lids at the idea and she quickly blinked them away, determined not to give Tony the satisfaction of seeing that he had upset her.

She picked up a towel and dried the dishes, using the few minutes to regather her composure round her like a protective shield. Over the past year she had learned to hide her feelings, learned to hide the pain and heartache behind a cool façade, and now she slipped it quietly back into place.

'Thanks for the advice, Tony. I'll bear it in mind. It's nice to know you have my welfare at heart.' Her voice was icy, tinged with a cutting sarcasm which brought a flush of anger to his heavy face. He straightened abruptly away from the door and walked out of the room and Kate breathed a sigh of relief. Gathering up the clean dishes, she stacked them neatly back in place, wondering why it hurt so much to realise what it was Aaron Blake probably wanted from her. No man had ever given her a reason to think well of him yet, so why should she have been foolish enough to think he was any different?

There was no sign of Aaron Blake the next day, or the next, or even the day after. Kate went about her work with an icy, imperturbable calm which even Tony's poisonous remarks couldn't penetrate. Oh, he tried, tried to prod and goad her into anger with his insults, his mocking comments to various customers in the café, but Kate felt as though she were cocooned in ice and that nothing, not even his barbs, could penetrate it.

She did her work then went back up to the flat and slept, and that was the sum total of her existence. Not that she wanted more, because she didn't. She just wanted to be left alone to rebuild her life in her own time and her own way. However, it seemed that life wasn't quite so willing to let her escape its clutches.

On the Friday of that strangely unsettling week two things happened almost simultaneously, two things which were to have a marked effect on her future. Aaron Blake suddenly walked into the café, and the telephone rang. Kate took just one look at his tall figure and turned away to snatch up the receiver, terrified of the wild feeling of elation which suddenly raced through her.

'Tony's Café.'

She clutched hold of the receiver in her shaking hand, gripping the cold, hard plastic in an attempt to stave off the wave of emotion which threatened to swamp her. Why had he come again? What did he want now? Could it be to see her again? Closing her eyes, she tried to get a grip of her emotions, to remember all Tony's mocking, taunting warnings, yet nothing could quell the rush of pleasure she felt at seeing him again.

'Hello? May I speak to Kate Warren, please?'

A man's voice came over the line, low, deep and somehow familiar, but for a blank second Kate couldn't place it.

'Speaking,' she replied, hesitantly.

'Thank heavens! I was afraid you wouldn't be there today, that it would be your day off or something. It's me, Kate . . . Jack.'

'Jack!'

Kate stared at the phone in surprise, wondering what could be so urgent that her brother-in-law had needed to call her about. He had never done it before, although Kate made a point of phoning Chrissie each weekend, just to reassure her that she was well.

'Are you still there?'

'Yes, sorry, Jack. I was just so surprised to hear——'

'Kate, listen! It's Chrissie, she's...' His voice broke and Kate felt a finger of icy fear trail slowly down her spine. She gripped hold of the wall with her free hand until her knuckles turned white from the pressure, trying to find the courage to ask the question she didn't want to ask. If anything had happened to Chrissie...

'What is it, Jack? Tell me! What's happened to her?'

There was silence and Kate felt herself grow even colder and shivered. Chrissie was seven months pregnant now, and she'd been so healthy up till now, so excited at the prospect of the coming baby. Please God that nothing had happened to spoil that happiness.

Jack drew in a deep breath, his voice shaking with pent-up emotion when he finally spoke. 'She's in hospital. From what I can make out she fell and knocked herself unconscious, but the doctors are still doing tests on her to see what other damage there is.'

'And the baby?' Kate could hardly speak, her whole body numb with shock.

'I don't know. They're monitoring him. There's a strong chance that the shock will send her into an early labour, but no one seems to be able to tell me anything definite yet. Oh, Kate, if you'd seen her, lying there when I came home and found her!'

A dry, rasping sob came over the line and Kate felt her eyes fill with tears as she heard it. Jack adored

Chrissie; she was his whole life and if anything happened to her he would be devastated.

'I...I'm sorry, Kate. I know that isn't going to help, but I feel so helpless!' He cleared his throat, obviously making an effort to get a grip on his emotions. 'Look, Kate, the doctors feel it's important that she's kept as quiet as possible. She's been asking for you and they think that it would help if you could come to see her just as soon as possible, to set her mind at rest. Will you?'

'Of course I will. Just give me all the details of where you are and I'll be there just as soon as I can.'

Snatching up a stub of pencil, she wrote the address down on her pad, her hand shaking so violently that the letters curled and slithered across the white sheet were almost indecipherable. 'Right, I've got that. I'm on my way, now, Jack. She'll be fine, you'll see. Chrissie is strong, a real fighter. You know she is.'

'I hope so, Kate. If anything happens to her I——' He broke off abruptly. 'I'll see you soon, Kate, and thank you. I know it will make all the difference having you here. You've always been so close.'

The line went dead and Kate slowly replaced the receiver, her face paper-white with shock and fear. She looked round, trying to think what to do next and where to go, but her mind was too numb to function properly. Chrissie couldn't die...she just couldn't! Not brave, loyal Chrissie, who'd battled to free her from prison, putting her own happiness at risk to save her. A sob rose to Kate's throat but she forced it down. She couldn't give in now, not when Chrissie needed her.

'Kate? What is it? What's happened?'

Aaron Blake came round the counter and took her hands in his, chafing the ice-cold flesh with his firm, hard fingers. 'Come on, sit down.'

He tried to ease her towards a nearby chair but Kate pulled away from him, lifting a trembling hand to push the silky wisps of red hair away from her temples as she tried to think. Almost blindly, she stared up at him, her eyes swimming with unshed tears.

'It's my sister, Chrissie. She's had an accident. She's in hospital and I've got to go to her.'

The words tumbled out all jumbled up but he seemed to understand what she meant because he nodded, his eyes filled with compassion. With a tiny start of surprise Kate realised that his eyes were blue, a deep, deep blue, so dark that they appeared almost black. How strange that she should notice such a detail at this moment. A slightly hysterical bubble of laughter rose up and she bit her lip to quell it.

'Where is your sister? Here in Liverpool?'

'No, she lives in London. I've got to get to her, but how?' She glanced at her watch, her eyes widening as she realised it was almost three o'clock. Even if she managed to catch a train in the next hour, it would be evening before she got to the hospital.

'I'll take you.'

'Pardon?'

For a second Kate stared at him in confusion. Hadn't he understood what she'd just said, that Chrissie was over two hundred miles away?

'I said I'll take you. I have a private plane at the airport. We can be there within the hour if we hurry.

I'll arrange for a car to meet us at the other end and take us on to the hospital.'

'Oh, but——'

'No buts, Kate. This is an emergency and there is no quicker way of getting there, believe me. Go and fetch your coat and then we can be on our way. I'll ring through to the airport and warn them.'

He gave her a little push towards the kitchen, his expression brooking no arguments, and Kate obeyed. Snatching her coat from the peg, she dragged it on, bemused by the speed of events.

'And just where do you think you're going?'

Standing at the table chopping onions, Tony glared at her, his face filled with an irritation which at any other time might have warned her to choose her words with caution. Now, however, Kate was far too worried about her sister to care what Tony would say about her sudden departure. She buttoned her coat, her fingers fumbling as they slid the buttons into place.

'My sister has had a bad accident. She's in hospital and I have to go to her. She's been asking for me.'

'Now? You really think that you can go wandering off right now, in the middle of the afternoon and leave me stranded? Well, you can just forget it! If you want to go visiting then you can wait until you're finished for the day. Now get your coat off and start on those pizzas before the teatime rush.'

Picking up the knife, Tony began to chop the onions again with sharp, vicious strokes which spoke volumes, but Kate stood her ground.

'I can't go tonight. Chrissie is in hospital in London. I have to go now.'

She picked up her bag and opened it to check if she had any money. All she could find was a couple of pounds and a handful of silver from the tips she'd been left during the week, but it would have to do. There was no time to go to the bank and cash a cheque.

'London! And how are you getting there?'

'Aaron Blake is taking me.'

The words came out before she could stop them and she felt her blood run cold as she saw the look which crossed Tony's face.

'So that's it, is it? You're going off with him. Well, it's up to you, Kate, but just one thing: if you go now then you needn't bother coming back!'

'But, Tony——'

'Ready, Kate? We'd better get going.'

Aaron Blake pushed the door open behind her, his eyes narrowing as he took in the scene, the way the air crackled with tension. 'Is there a problem?' he asked, moving further into the room, his eyes running from one still figure to the other.

'Yes, you could say that,' Tony snapped back, tossing the knife down so that the blade embedded itself in the chopping board. 'There's a problem for Kate if she leaves now. She needn't bother coming back because there will be no job here for her.'

'Hasn't she explained about her sister's accident?' Cold contempt laced Blake's deep voice and Tony's face went livid as he heard it.

'Oh, she explained all right. Nice touching little story it was too. How long did it take you to make it up? OK, if you want Kate then have her, but on your

time not mine. I don't pay her to go making a bit on
the side with any man who takes her fancy!'

The two men glared at each other and Kate looked
at them, feeling sick. She had known for weeks now
that Tony had it in for her, but she'd never quite
realised just how bitter he felt. How could he have
said that about her? She swung round, knowing she
couldn't bear to stay in the same room with him a
moment longer.

'Remember, Kate, if you walk out of here now then
you needn't bother coming back. You're finished!'

Tony's voice followed her across the café but she
didn't even hesitate as she walked out of the door.
She might regret the loss of her job later, might rue
the fact that she hadn't tried to make him understand, but right at that moment she didn't give a damn
about Tony Manetti, or his café, or his rotten job!
All that really mattered now was Chrissie.

CHAPTER THREE

'THIS way. My car's down here.'

Aaron Blake took her arm to steer her down the street, and Kate was suddenly grateful for the firm support of his hand as her legs started to tremble with reaction. That scene on top of the news about Chrissie had been the final straw. How could Tony have said that, made a show of her in that fashion? She didn't know, couldn't understand how anyone could be so heartlessly cruel. Still, what did it matter now? Now she had to concentrate on Chrissie, and doing all she could to help her.

Just how badly hurt was she? Jack had said that she had fallen, but where and how? How much damage had she done to herself and her unborn child? Kate drew in a ragged breath as she tried to stem the rising tide of panic which threatened to engulf her as she considered the possibilities, unaware of the sideways glance Aaron Blake shot at her, or the way his eyes darkened as he saw the strain etched on her white face. He stopped abruptly and swung her round, his fingers biting deep into her flesh.

'Stop it, Kate! Stop torturing yourself like this. I'm sure your sister will be fine.'

'Will she? Oh, I hope so, I really hope so!'

The plea whispered from her, shaky with a need for reassurance as she stared up into his hard-boned face, and with a low oath he pulled her to him, pressing her trembling body against the hard length of his own. He lifted his hand, smoothing the silky cap of red hair, a hesitant, reluctant tenderness in his eyes as he watched the way it clung to his fingers like tongues of fire.

For a few moments Kate rested against him, deriving comfort from the feel of his hard, strong body pressed against hers. Then slowly she eased away, her eyes a deep cloudy green as she stared up into his face. Despite everything that Tony had said, there was little doubt that Aaron Blake was genuinely concerned and wanted to help her. He might have other reasons for coming to the café and talking to her, reasons she didn't understand, but right at that moment she could believe that he really wanted to help her. She could see it in the level darkness of his gaze and in the quiet strength of his face.

The realisation steadied her, gave her the strength to fight against the numbing chill of fear. In some way she could almost believe that Chrissie would be all right because he had said so.

'All right now?' he asked quietly and Kate nodded gravely.

He held his hand out and slowly she slid her fingers into his, feeling strangely protected and cared for as his hand closed warmly round hers. In silence they walked the rest of the way to where he'd left his car, a sleek dark sports model which looked oddly out of place in the run-down area. He pulled the keys out of his pocket and unlocked the door, helping her inside before crossing the pavement to where two youths were standing huddled in a doorway, their shoulders hunched against the cold chill of the icy wind.

As Kate watched, he pulled out his wallet and peeled off a note, handing it over to the boys before striding back to the car and climbing inside. He slipped the key into the ignition, shooting a smile at her as he saw the questioning look on her face.

'My minders,' he said briefly.

'Minders! What on earth do you mean?'

'We struck a deal last week, you see. They would mind the car and ensure that nothing . . . nasty happened to it, if I agreed to pay them a fee. As I had no desire to come back and find the windscreen smashed it seemed like a sensible arrangement.'

'Sensible! Why, it sounds like extortion to me,' Kate said in horror, staring out of the window at the retreating figures. 'If you hadn't agreed to their demands then obviously they would have done something to the car themselves.'

'Most probably,' he agreed easily. 'But let's not call it extortion, shall we? That seems a bit hard. How about free enterprise? After all, I can remember doing much the same thing myself when I was their age, or even younger.'

'You did?' For a second Kate stared at him, her eyes mirroring her surprise as they swept over his expensively clad figure, the almost tangible aura of wealth which surrounded him. 'I don't believe it! Why on earth would you do such a thing?'

'Same reason as they do, I imagine: money. I haven't always been rich, Kate' he said tersely, his mouth tightening as though in remembrance of something disturbing. 'I grew up in an area very similar to this one, though it was in London not Liverpool, and I learned very early on how to make a living any way I could. I just went on to develop that talent, that's all. I might have all the trappings of wealth now, and all the gloss to varnish over the rough edges, but underneath I'm still the same person who knew what it was like to be out on the street and fighting to make ends meet.'

He pulled out into the traffic and Kate sat silently mulling over what he'd just told her. In one way it was hard to imagine this man had ever had to fight for anything, yet in another it was all too easy. Aaron Blake might be the epitome of the rich, suave businessman, but there was an innate hardness behind that sleek façade. She only had to remember what had happened in the café, how he had handled that ruffian who'd tried to maul her, to know he could cope with even the toughest situation. There was more to this man than met the eyes—far more!

The idea was disturbing. Was she too making the mistake of seeing the façade and not what lay behind it? Did Aaron Blake have some other, far less altruistic reason for helping her? Panic reared its ugly head as Kate weighed up the situation, wondering if she'd been crazy to entrust herself to a total stranger. Why, for all she knew he could be planning anything, anything at all, and here she was calmly going along with it!

'Relax, Kate. Stop getting yourself so worked up. There's nothing to worry about.'

'Isn't there?' She turned sideways, studying his hard-cut profile. 'Why are you doing this, Mr Blake?

Why are you going out of your way to help me like this?'

'Maybe I just enjoy playing the Good Samaritan,' he said easily, flicking her a swift glance.

Kate studied him, her eyes lingering on the hard bones and angles of his face, the glittering darkness of his eyes, and shook her head slowly.

'No...no, I don't believe that's why.' She shrugged, a trace of colour stealing under her skin as he raised a quizzical brow. 'I don't know much about you, Mr Blake, apart from what I read in the paper, but somehow I don't get the impression that you're the sort of person who makes a habit of playing the Good Samaritan!'

'Are any of us what we seem, Kate? Are you?'

'What do you mean?'

An icy chill raced through her body at the harsh note in his voice and unconsciously she hugged her arms tightly round her to stem the betraying shudder.

'Well, you look so sweetly innocent, but are you really, Kate? Are you as unmarked by life as you appear to be?'

If only she were! Kate swallowed down the fervent wish, realising she mustn't utter the words aloud and arouse his suspicions. It was difficult to know what he was getting at, difficult to see where this strangely unsettling conversation was leading to, but she sensed a certain purpose behind the seemingly casual question, a coiled tension about him as he waited for her to answer.

She forced a laughing note to her voice, hoping he couldn't hear the unease which was rippling through her. 'Is anyone? Let's just say that my conscience is clear.'

'Is it, Kate? Is it really?'

There was no doubting the tone of his voice now, and Kate sat up straighter and met his probing gaze squarely.

'Yes,' she repeated, her soft voice tinged with sincerity. 'My conscience is quite clear.'

For a moment he studied her, then looked away, turning his attention back to the traffic. Kate slumped back in her seat feeling exhausted, as though she had just completed number one in Hercules' twelve labours...and won! Lord knew if she'd ever find the strength to cope with number two!

Within half an hour they arrived at the airport and Blake parked the car before leaving Kate to check if the plane was ready. Kate stared round, her eyes following a tiny two-seater plane which was making its way towards the runway, wondering what sort of a plane they would be flying in. Hopefully nothing as small and fragile-looking as that!

'Right, we're ready. We can take off in about ten minutes, so let's get on board, shall we?'

Aaron Blake appeared and took her arm to steer her round the side of a hangar, smiling as he heard her stifled gasp of amazement as she suddenly spotted the sleek silver plane parked on the apron. With its elegant lines and the legend Blake International emblazoned on its side in brilliant scarlet, it was as far removed from the tiny two-seater as a duck from a swan, and Kate couldn't hide her astonishment.

'Like it?' he asked, openly laughing at her expression.

'I . . . well, yes! I just never expected anything like this!' Unbidden, her eyes turned towards the other plane which was just taking off, poised in that instant of time when it had to fight the pull of gravity to take to the skies.

'Oh, I think we can do better than that, a lot better, in fact. You'll be more than comfortable on this flight. Now come along and let's get on board.'

He led the way across the tarmac and Kate followed him in a dream, still stunned by the sight of the expensive and luxurious machine. At the bottom of the steps there was a middle-aged man in a dark uniform waiting to greet them. He shook Aaron Blake's hand then turned to smile at Kate, a hint of curiosity in the look he ran over her from top to toe. Suddenly Kate came back to earth with a jolt and stood up straighter, quelling the urge to run a hand over her wind-tousled red hair, and glad that she was wearing the dark tweed coat which still bore the hall-marks of good tailoring. It was a couple of years old now, but the cut and quality of the cloth were un-mistakable and she was glad that she wasn't letting her side down! Undoubtedly the women who usually accompanied Aaron Blake in this sleek machine were always immaculately dressed, but at least Kate had the satisfaction of knowing that the dark olive colour of the coat and the elegantly simple lines made the most of her rich red hair and slender figure. She mightn't have been able to save much from her former life, but what she had had been worth keeping!

Within minutes they were seated and Kate fastened her seatbelt, her hands fumbling slightly with the unfamiliar strap and buckle. Aaron Blake leant over and took it from her, fastening the clasp with deft fingers.

'You're not nervous about flying, are you, Kate? I never thought to ask before, but there is really no need to worry. Brian is a first-class pilot. He's been with the company for several years now.'

He was watching her closely and Kate forced a smile to her lips to cover the confusion she felt at his closeness.

'No, not at all. I like flying, though this is something very new to me. I've never been on a private plane before.'

'But you have flown before?'

He sat back, shifting round to make himself more comfortable, his long legs brushing against hers. Kate felt a sudden flare of awareness shoot through her at the contact and looked down, frightened that he would see how much he disturbed her. Since Jonathan and the whole sordid nightmare of the trial she'd felt nothing for any man, so why did she feel these strange tingling sensations whenever Aaron Blake touched her? It wasn't as if he was exceptionally handsome, although his hard-boned face held a rugged attraction which would draw any woman's eyes. Yet something about him attracted her and made her feel more aware of him as a man than she'd felt of anyone before.

Confused by the sudden realisation, Kate answered the question without really thinking what she was doing.

'Yes. I flew to America last year.'

'America, indeed? Well, this trip will be child's play after that. Where did you stay?'

There was curiosity on his face and Kate felt herself grow cold as she realised what she'd done. Why had she said that? It had been so stupid, arousing his curiosity about her, and that was the very last thing she wanted to do. She didn't want him asking questions she had no wish to answer.

'New York. It was just a short trip, only three days, in fact, so I didn't see that much of the city.'

Biting her lip, Kate prayed that her brief little answer would dampen his interest, but of course it didn't. If anything, it seemed to make him more interested than ever!

'Oh, so was it a business trip, then, not a holiday?'

A business trip! A wave of bitter, hysterical laughter rose inside her as she heard the question. She turned away to stare out of the window, desperately trying to control it.

It had been in New York where it had all begun. New York where she had gone to meet Jonathan, believing that the trip would mark a new phase in their relationship. Well, it had done that all right, but not in the way she'd imagined!

It had been in New York where he had put the consignment of drugs into her luggage after telling her that it was a present he had promised to bring back for a friend. And she, in her love-blind innocence, had believed him. He had used her from start to finish, used the love she felt for him with a blatant ruthless disregard. He had taken everything from her: her love, her hopes, all those foolish tender dreams of the life they would build together, and destroyed them. She would never think of that city again without a feeling of cold dread.

'Kate?'

There was a questioning note in Aaron's voice and Kate drew in a ragged breath, knowing she had to answer him. She turned back, her face set and etched with a grief she was unaware of.

'No, the trip wasn't for business. I went there to meet a friend.'

'I see.'

His voice was expressionless, yet Kate had the strangest feeling that something had angered him— but what? Unless he'd realised that the friend was a man, and then added two and two and come up with entirely the wrong conclusion. Perhaps Tony's words had stuck in his mind more than she'd realised. After all, here she was, a low-paid waitress, so was it any wonder that he should assume the worst and believe that some man had paid for the trip for the most obvious of reasons?

Anger rippled through her at the thought of how he was misjudging her, adding fire to her eyes and ice to her voice.

'I know exactly what you are thinking. But you're wrong. I don't sell myself to anyone, and definitely not for the price of a plane ticket! Now I think it would be better if you let me off this plane right now, don't you? I'd hate to think you had the wrong idea and were expecting something more than a few words of thanks at the end of the journey, because you are going to be disappointed!' She unbuckled the belt and

stood up, her body rigid with barely controlled anger.
'Excuse me.'

'Sit down, Kate.'

'I don't want to sit down, I want to get off this plane!'

'I'm afraid it's a bit too late for that. We're about to take off.' He swept a hand towards the window and Kate could see that they were starting to inch their way forwards across the grey tarmac.

'Surely you can stop it, can't you?' she demanded, glaring at him.

'If I wanted to, yes, but I don't. So sit down and stop making a complete fool of yourself.'

He caught her hand and jerked her back down to the seat, his hard fingers biting into her flesh as he held her down while he refastened the belt. Kate struggled against his grip, twisting her arm, but he only held her tighter, his face darkening with anger.

'Stop it, woman. Stop it now!'

The command stopped her dead. Kate glared mutinously at him but he ignored her, sitting back in his seat as the belt snapped into place. His face was coldly remote, all traces of warmth gone from his dark eyes as he flicked a glance at her before looking away. Kate felt all the anger drain from her as quickly as it had come. She glanced down at her hands, lying clenched in her lap, then back at him, hating to see such indifference on his face.

'I'm sorry.'

Her words were almost swallowed up by the sudden roar of the engines, but he must have caught them. He looked sideways at her, his face still set, and she shivered, hating him looking at her that way. Reaching out, she laid her hand on his in a mute appeal for forgiveness, and suddenly his expression softened. He took her hand, pressing her fingers for a brief second.

'You're quite wrong, Kate. I don't expect anything like that for helping you. I'm sorry if I gave you that impression.'

'I know, and I'm sorry, for saying such a thing when you've been so kind. It was quite uncalled for.' She gave a cold little laugh. 'I suppose I'm just not used to people wanting to help me, that's all. It would be so much easier if I just understood why you've done it, why you should go to so much trouble to help me, a virtual stranger.'

She studied him, searching his face for all the answers to all the questions which were racing through her head, but there was little to be read in his expression.

He shrugged as he let her hand go, staring past her out of the window. 'You needed help and I happened to be there and able to give it. There's no great mystery about it, Kate. Anyone would have done the same in my position.'

Would they? Kate doubted that, doubted that anyone would have gone to this amount of trouble, yet what else could she say? How could she press him further without appearing rude and ungrateful? After all, what did it really matter why Aaron Blake had helped her? When they reached London it was highly unlikely that she would ever see him again. The thought was oddly depressing.

* * *

The hospital was quiet, a faint, cool smell of antiseptic lingering in the silent corridors which made Kate feel slightly sick. She clung hold of Aaron's hand as he led her along the maze of corridors, feeling intensely glad that he had ignored her assurances that she could manage and insisted on coming with her.

Far from leaving her at the airport as she'd expected him to do, he had organised everything down to the last detail, from the smooth, swift flight across the country to the sleek fast car waiting at the airport to rush them to the hospital. Left to her own devices, Kate knew she would never have been able to complete the journey in such a rapid time, and she was immeasurably grateful to him. It was a debt she would owe him for the rest of her life, and one which she hoped she'd be able to repay some day.

'Here we are. This looks like the room.'

He reached past her to push the waiting-room door open but Kate hesitated, her feet glued to the spot in sudden fear. At this final moment her courage had quite deserted her.

'Kate?' He swung round, his eyes tracing over her pale face, the tremble of her bloodless lips, and something flashed in his eyes, a flicker of emotion so quickly gone that she barely had time to recognise its passing. He caught hold of her arms, his fingers firm as they closed round her flesh.

'Come on, Kate,' he said softly. 'You can do it. Don't let her down, not now. You've got to be brave now for both of you, sweetheart.'

Kate closed her eyes, swallowing down the sob which had risen to her throat, the stabbing chill of icy fear for what she would find on the other side of that door. She took a slow, deep breath and walked slowly past him into the quiet dimness of the room.

'Kate!' The hushed murmur of surprise echoed through the silence and Kate made the supreme effort of her life and summoned up a smile for the tall man standing by the window.

'Hello, Jack. How is she?'

'I don't know. They haven't let me see her yet. A nurse came in about an hour ago and told me that she'd regained consciousness but since then I've heard nothing. It's slowly driving me crazy!' His voice broke and he turned away, rubbing a shaking hand over his face, his shoulders hunched as he stared blindly out of the window.

With a tiny murmur Kate crossed the room and threw her arms round him, her own eyes wet with a sudden flood of tears.

'She'll be all right, Jack. She will. You know Chrissie, she's tough. In a couple of hours she'll be fine and bossing us about all over the place.'

'Will she? Lord, I hope so, Kate. If you'd just seen her lying there on the floor like a crumpled doll . . .' There was agony in his deep voice at the memory and Kate held him harder, desperate to ease the cutting edge of his fear.

'Have they run any tests on her yet, do you know?' Aaron Blake moved quietly further into the room, his voice level, cutting through the emotional tension.

Kate felt Jack stiffen before he turned towards him, a faintly hostile look in his eyes as they ran over Blake's tall, elegant figure.

For a moment Kate studied the two men, her eyes roving from one to the other, seeing the differences and strangely enough the similarities. Somehow she'd not realised before that they were alike.

Both were tall and dark-haired, though Jack with his heavier build and extra inches had the edge in that respect. Yet both had that same indefinable aura of toughness, that air of authority which seemed to sit so easily on their shoulders. It set them apart from other men, made them stand head and shoulders above the crowd.

The realisation flashed through Kate's head like summer lightning, brief and vivid, then suddenly she became aware of the fact that both men were looking at her, Aaron with something akin to amusement in his eyes and Jack with definite annoyance. She hurried to introduce them, smiling placatingly at her brother-in-law as she performed the task. Jack had a tendency to be very protective of her; he was probably wondering just who Aaron was and what he was doing at the hospital with her.

'Jack, I'd like you to meet Aaron Blake. He very kindly flew me down here in his plane and arranged for a car to bring us to the hospital. Mr Blake . . . my brother-in-law, Jackson Knight.'

She watched while the two men shook hands, obviously weighing each other up, her breath suddenly tight in her chest as she waited to see Jack's reaction to the other man. Suddenly, it seemed terribly important that he should set his seal of approval on Aaron Blake.

'Mr Blake. I must thank you. It was good of you to help Kate like that. We all appreciate it.'

'It was my pleasure. I only hope that your wife will make a swift recovery soon. What have the doctors done so far? What have they said?'

Jack ran a hand through his hair, ruffling the dark strands as he must have done a hundred times that day. 'Not much so far. You know what they're like, very cagey. They want to wait for the results of the tests before they commit themselves. I only hope that——'

He broke off abruptly, his body tensing, as a nurse opened the door and came into the room. She glanced round, a faint surprise on her face as she saw Kate and Aaron Blake, before she turned to Jack.

'Mr Knight, the doctor has said that you can go in to see your wife now as long as you only stay for a few minutes. She's still rather groggy, but she absolutely refuses to settle down until she has seen you. However, the good news is that all the tests we've run point to the fact that there's been no lasting damage done. She's going to feel rather bruised and sore for the next few days and will need complete rest, but hopefully everything will be fine.'

Jack closed his eyes, his lips moving in a silent prayer of thanks. 'Thank you, Nurse. That's the best news I've heard in the whole of my life!'

The nurse smiled, her eyes filled with understanding. 'I had the feeling it might be. Now if you'll just come with me...oh, by the way, is there any news about Mrs Knight's sister yet? She's been asking for her again and the doctor feels certain that it would be an enormous help if she could see her.'

Kate stepped hurriedly forwards, feeling almost weak from relief at the news. 'I'm Kate Warren, nurse, Mrs Knight's sister.'

'Oh, good. Well, I don't see any reason why you can't both go in to see her together. It would ease her mind and that's the main thing we want to do right now. She needs to be kept as calm as possible. If you'll both follow me.'

She led the way from the waiting-room with Jack hard on her heels, but Kate hesitated. She looked at Aaron, who was standing quietly by the window.

'Will you...?'

She stopped, wondering if she really had the right to ask him to wait. It seemed such an impertinence to ask for yet more of his time, but she didn't want him to leave and disappear into the night. She wanted to thank him properly for all he'd done in getting her to the hospital and, if she was really honest, find out if she would ever see him again. Yet how could she ask that apparently simple question, and ask more of him than he might be willing to give?

In a quandary, Kate fell silent, her green eyes filled with the questions she couldn't voice. He smiled at her, his voice strangely reassuring when he spoke.

'Go along, Kate. I'll still be here when you get back.'

The words sounded almost like a promise and Kate couldn't hide the sudden rush of pleasure she felt. She hurried from the room, missing the fleeting hint of regret which crossed his face as he stared after her retreating figure.

CHAPTER FOUR

IT WAS raining, a thin, fine mist of rain which felt deliciously cool and fresh after the stuffy overheated atmosphere inside the hospital. Kate walked down the shallow flight of steps from the main door, turning her face up to the cool spray, savouring its freshness, the feeling of release.

It was almost ten p.m. and she'd been in the hospital for several hours, determined to stay with Jack and keep him company in his vigil. However, in the past hour when it had become apparent that Chrissie's condition was increasingly stable, she had agreed to go and get some rest. It made sense, of course, that one of them should get some sleep then take over from the other in the morning, but she had been reluctant to leave until Aaron had added his voice to Jack's. Somehow it had been incredibly difficult to argue with him, to fight against the cool, clear logic in his deep voice, and, finally, Kate had given up the battle.

Headlights cut through the dark, coming slowly towards her from the direction of the car park, and Kate drew in a slow deep breath, feeling her heart start to race in sudden panic. Without really consulting her, Jack and Aaron had calmly made arrangements for her to spend the night at Aaron Blake's house in the city, brushing aside her protests that she could find a room somewhere. Aaron Blake's voice had been flatly level as he'd explained that his house-keeper would be there, yet Kate could still feel a tiny flutter of unease racing through her at the thought of spending the night with him, no matter who was there to act as chaperon!

'Ready, Kate? Jump in.'

Aaron leant across to swing the car door open for her, his face looking harshly unfamiliar in the eerie glow from the dashboard, and Kate stepped back a pace, her heart pounding like a wild thing. She glanced up and down the near-deserted driveway, wondering how on earth she could ease herself out of the predicament gracefully.

'Kate? What's the matter? You know you can't stay here all night. You're exhausted.' His voice held just the slightest note of impatience and Kate cast round desperately for some sort of an excuse.

'I...well, I really think it would be better if I stayed, you know. I mean, Jack might need me or Chrissie might wake up and ask for me again...and, really, I don't want to put you to all this trouble. You've done more than enough already.'

It sounded lame even to her own ears, her trembling voice betraying more about what she really meant than she'd intended, and Kate felt the colour surge to her cheeks as he laughed in mocking disbelief.

'And that's why you now want to stay, is it? Not because you've suddenly got cold feet? Listen, Kate, I promise you that you'll be quite safe. All I'm offering is *a* bed for the night, not *my* bed, so stop worrying. Anyway, I don't know about you but I'm starving. The only thing I'm lusting after tonight is food . . . nothing else!'

He revved the engine and Kate slid quickly into the car, her face flaming with embarrassment and a tiny measure of annoyance. Did he have to make it sound quite so ridiculous, as though no man in his right mind would ever want her? Gently seething, she stared silently straight ahead out of the windscreen, refusing to turn her head and look at him.

'Don't sulk, Kate. It doesn't suit you.'

'I am not sulking,' she said sharply. 'I never sulk!'

'No? Well, I'd say you're giving a pretty good imitation of it now. What exactly is bothering you most: the thought of spending the night under my roof, or the fact that I'm more interested in my dinner right now than your charms?'

Kate gasped in indignation and rounded on him, refusing to admit even to herself that he was right. 'Of course I'm not annoyed about that! Don't be silly. I just didn't want to put you to any more trouble tonight, that's all.'

'Well, don't worry about it any further. I've a whole house full of empty bedrooms, all ready and waiting in case someone stays over. There's no problem.'

He slipped the car into gear and drove slowly out of the hospital gates, and Kate leant back in her seat, knowing she had been outmanoeuvred. What else could she say without making herself look even more foolish? She closed her eyes and turned her head away, feigning sleep while she seethed gently at the easy way he had handled her. Yet, gradually, as the car drove smoothly on, she found herself relaxing. There was something hypnotically soothing about the rhythmic flicker of street lamps against her closed lids, the soft, steady beat of the windscreen wipers, and she was so tired. Suddenly all the anger and emotions she'd experienced that day caught up with her and she drifted into a light sleep.

When the car turned sharply into the driveway of Aaron Blake's house and came to an abrupt halt she woke with a jolt. Her heart was thumping, her mouth dry, and she swallowed hard as she stared round trying to orientate herself, but there was little she could see. The whole place was in darkness and a flicker of unease raced up her spine as she shot a questioning look at the man sitting silently next to her.

'I thought you said your housekeeper would be here. The place looks deserted to me.'

'I did and so she should be. I don't know what's going on but I want you to stay right here, Kate, just in case I run into any trouble. I don't like the look of this at all.'

Grim-faced, he climbed out of the car and strode towards the house. He unlocked the front door and disappeared inside, leaving Kate staring after him in apprehension. What if something *had* happened? She couldn't leave Aaron to face it all on his own.

She climbed out of the car and hurried after him, pausing uncertainly just inside the doorway. The house was quiet, not a whisper of sound or a flicker of movement issuing from any direction, so it was hard to know which way she should go to find Aaron. Obviously he had decided not to switch the lights on but Kate found the inky, almost impenetrable darkness

unnerving. There was something terrifying about
standing on the threshold of this silent house, unable
to see more than a few feet in front of her, which
filled her with primeval fear.

'What the hell——?'

The sudden exclamation followed by a loud crash
galvanised her into action. Following the direction of
the sound, Kate raced across the hall and flung a door
open, then screamed in terror as a dark shape hurled
itself towards her and sent her crashing to the floor.
Breathless, shaken, she lay on the carpet, her body
trapped beneath a crushing weight, too stunned by
the speed of the attack to even scream for help. Suddenly the weight was lifted, lights flared and she drew
in a slow, shaky breath of relief as she stared up at
the man who towered over her, his face grim.

'Kate! Why on earth didn't you stay in the car as
I told you to?' He knelt down and lifted her into a
sitting position, supporting her against his shoulder
as she struggled to suck enough air back into her lungs
to speak. She smiled at him, a shaky little smile which
changed to a grimace as she ran a hand gingerly over
the back of her head. Despite the thick carpet, she'd
hit the floor with such a bump that there was a huge
lump forming on the back of her skull, and she winced
as her probing fingers brushed against it.

'I...I was worried about you,' she managed at last,
panting slightly. 'I thought you might need some help.'

'Help? Are you mad, Kate? What could you have
done to help me even if I had run into trouble? You
should have done as I said and stayed in the car rather

than come in here and risk getting yourself hurt like this, you crazy woman!'

How dared he? She pulled away and staggered unsteadily to her feet, feeling both furious and strangely hurt by his reaction. She'd only wanted to help, after all. So did he really need to be so horrible about it and call her names? She smoothed her clothes down, her hands shaking in sudden reaction. This on top of everything else which had happened that day was the final straw and she turned away as an un-expected sob racked her body.

'Kate! Oh, hell, I'm sorry. I didn't mean to snap like that.'

Aaron stepped in front of her and attempted to pull her into his arms, but she resisted with a strength which surprised them both. She glared up at him, her face wet with tears, her green eyes sparkling with a mixture of anger and hurt.

'Don't touch me! I don't want your apologies, Aaron Blake,' she hiccuped defiantly through the tears. 'All I wanted to do was help you. There was no need for you to start calling me names!'

'I know. I'm sorry, Kate, really I am. But when I realised it was you on the floor, and how I could have hurt you…well——' He broke off, anguish in his eyes as he stared down at her tear-stained face. 'I'm sorry, Kate.'

He ran his hands up her arms, his touch so light, so exquisitely tender, that Kate felt the very last thread of control snap. She bent her head, resting it against the warmly comforting strength of his shoulder as she gave in to the sudden flood of emotion.

'Don't, Kate . . . don't.'

Almost roughly, he pulled her to him, pressing her head deeper into his shoulder as he held her against his body, and Kate sobbed even harder. Ever since she'd found out about Jonathan, and finally faced up to the fact of how he had deceived her, she'd held her emotions in check. Now, however, the barriers had been broken, and all the pain and hurt of the past year came flooding out.

Kate never knew how long they stood like that, but when finally the tears began to abate she felt as though a huge great weight had been lifted off her shoulders. She felt drained, yet free—as though life might one day have some meaning for her again.

'Better now?'

Tilting her chin, Aaron studied her ravaged face with darkened eyes, and with a sudden rush of embarrassment Kate realised what a sight she must look. She brushed the last tears from her damp cheeks, then forced a smile to her lips.

'Yes. I'm sorry. I didn't mean to make such a show of myself. I must look a mess.'

She went to step back, shooting a startled glance upwards when he continued to hold on to her, and felt her breath catch sharply as she saw the expression on his face. Suddenly her heart began to hammer in fast, nervous spurts, sending the blood rushing hotly through her veins.

'You could never look anything but beautiful, Kate,' he said quietly, his voice so deep that a delicious shiver inched its way up her spine.

For a moment he stared down into her startled face, then slowly, so slowly, bent his head, and Kate closed her eyes as she waited for the touch of his lips against hers. He was so close that she could feel the warmth of his breath mist on her damp eyelids, could smell the faint, intoxicating aroma of cologne which clung to his skin. In that instant, Kate knew that she wanted nothing more from life than to feel the magic of this man's kiss.

The harsh, discordant sound of the telephone broke the spell. Kate shivered, brought back to reality with a cruel speed as Aaron cursed and let her go before hurrying to answer it. She wrapped her arms tightly round her body to quell the trembles which coursed through her, then looked round the room, fighting for her composure.

It was a beautiful room, and as her eyes lingered on the expensive furniture, the rich fabrics, the luxuries which spoke of wealth, she felt an icy coldness invade her limbs. This room, this whole house, was that of a rich, successful man, so what could he possibly want with a woman like her? Those few minutes in his arms had been magical, but she had to face up to life as it was and not as she wanted it to be. Aaron Blake might have wanted to kiss her just now, but hadn't it been because he'd felt sorry for distressing her, and because she'd been in his arms, ready and very obviously willing to let him? She would be foolish to let herself believe that it was for any other reason. He must have his pick of beautiful, equally successful women, so why should he be interested in a penniless little nobody like her?

He walked back into the room and Kate drew the cloak of cool composure round her once again as she turned to face him. Inside she might be aching but she would never show it, never let him see how much that brief interlude had meant to her. She couldn't . . . *wouldn't*, let herself be vulnerable to any man again!

'That was Mrs Baker, my housekeeper. She'd rung the hotel where I've been staying and they'd informed her that I'd returned home. She just wanted to remind me that she'll be away on holiday for the next couple of weeks. She quite rightly guessed that I would forget all about it. I'm sorry, Kate, but this does seem to give us an added problem, doesn't it?'

'What do you mean?'

'Well, let's be blunt, you were uneasy about staying here even with Mrs Baker on the premises, so how do you feel about it now? Obviously, you have my word that you'll be quite safe, but I do understand if you'd prefer not to stay.' He glanced at his watch, a frown darkening his brow as he looked back at her. 'It could be awkward, but I suppose there is just a chance that I'll be able to find you a room in a hotel tonight, but you'll have to let me know what you want to do immediately. I don't fancy tramping the streets well into the early hours.'

There was silence while he waited for her answer, and Kate could hear the sudden thunderous pounding of her heart and wondered if he could hear it too. Should she stay or should she insist on finding a hotel room? A simple decision which should be based on common sense and the certainty that she shouldn't get herself too deeply involved with this man. Yet how could she insist he set off now, at this time of the night, to find her a room? He'd done so much already for her today; could she really ask him to do more and put him to even more trouble?

'I'll stay, if you're sure it's no bother. Thank you.'

'Good.'

He crossed the room and took her hands, and Kate had the sudden craziest feeling that there was relief in his eyes as he stared down at her for a brief moment, but why? Why should it matter to him that she was willing to stay at his house?

The question slid into her mind then slid out again just as quickly as he bent and brushed a light kiss against her cheek. Kate held herself rigid, fighting down the sudden urge to wrap her arms round his neck and kiss him back. Aaron had been a friend to her today in the true meaning of the word, and that was exactly how she must think of him. It would be too easy to let herself get carried away by wishful thoughts and foolish fancies. And she knew to her cost how dangerous that could be!

It was still raining when Kate awoke the next morning. She huddled deeper into the soft bed, burrowing under the thick blankets as she savoured the feeling of warmth and comfort, the knowledge that this morning, at least, she wouldn't have to jump up and spend ten hours on her feet waiting tables or suffer any more of Tony's coarse comments. She hadn't realised before just how much she had come to dread each new day until now when she didn't have to face it. She might be out of a job and probably homeless, but surely she could find something better than what she'd been putting up with?

Suddenly uneasy about what the future might bring, she jumped out of bed and shivered as the cool morning air flowed over her warm skin. Not wanting to ruin the one set of clothes she had with her, she had slept only in her bra and panties. Now, however, she would have been grateful for something more substantial than the delicate wisps of lace and satin. She glanced round the room, her eyes narrowing as she wondered if she dared investigate the contents of the wardrobes to find a robe, before shrugging the idea aside as pointless. With the bathroom adjoining the bedroom, what on earth did she need a robe for? She could be showered and dressed in no time.

She hurried across the room and flung the bathroom door open, gasping in dismay as she found Aaron Blake already in there...totally naked! For one long, timeless moment she stood rooted to the spot as her eyes swept from the top of his sleek, wet head to the damp tips of his well-shaped toes, then slammed the door again. Closing her eyes, she leant weakly back against the door as she drew in breath after breath of much needed air, but nothing as mundane as deep breathing seemed able to calm the heavy sickening pounding of her heart. Just the memory of him standing there, his body gleaming in the pale golden glow of the overhead light made her feel dizzy. Why oh, why hadn't she thought to knock instead of barging in like that? She would never be able to face him again...never!

A light tapping at the door behind her made her jump. Kate leapt away from it as though it had suddenly been shot through with an electric current. She raised a trembling hand to her throat to calm the wildly beating pulse and forced herself to answer, though little more than a whispering croak issued from her lips.

'Yes? What is it?'

'Bathroom's free now if you want it. Sorry if I gave you a fright just now. I never thought to lock the door. Habit, I guess.'

Fright! Well, maybe that hadn't been quite her reaction to finding him there if she was really truthful, but right at that moment Kate wasn't up to being truthful even to herself! Her reaction to the sight of Aaron standing there like a gleaming, carved statue had stemmed from something other than fright, but she had no intention of admitting it! She grasped the lifeline he had thrown her and clung grimly on, weathering the inward storm of emotions.

'That's all right. You...you startled me, that's all.'

'Sorry. Oh, by the way, there's a robe in one of those wardrobes. Shall I come in and find it for you?'

The door-handle started to turn and Kate cast desperate eyes at it before leaping forwards and leaning her full weight against the cold wooden panels.

'No! I mean, no, thank you. There's no need to trouble yourself on my account. I'll manage, really. I . . . I don't need a robe.' She was gabbling, the words tumbling out in a nervous frothy torrent. The last thing she wanted was for Aaron to come into the room . . . naked!

He laughed, the sound echoing deeply through the tightly closed door, and she flinched nervously.

'I *am* wearing something now, Kate, you know. I'm not in the habit of walking in and out of guests' rooms stark naked.'

Put like that it sounded so ridiculous that Kate felt her cheeks burn with fresh heat. However, there was still no way she wanted him in here, not with her clad only in these skimpy little bits of nothing. She might have had an uncensored view of him, but his view of her must have been only fractionally less revealing, and she had no intention of giving him a second showing!

'It's quite all right, really.'

'Well, please yourself. Come down when you're ready, Kate. I'll put some coffee on.'

There was the soft but distinct sound of a door closing on the far side of the bathroom but Kate still hesitated, loath to go back into the room until she was sure the coast was completely clear. She huddled against the door, pressing her ear to the wood until finally the shivering chills racing through her body spurred her into action. If she didn't get showered and dressed soon then she was in real danger of catching pneumonia.

Easing the door open just the barest fraction, she peered into the bathroom, but apart from a few clinging wisps of steam and a faint delicate smell of cologne it was empty. She hurried inside and hastily bolted the door on the opposite side, taking no chances on Aaron's walking back in and catching *her*. One shock per day was quite enough for anyone's system.

She stepped into the shower stall and turned on the water to full power, letting it pour hotly over her head and shoulders and bring warmth back to her cold limbs. There was a bar of soap in the wall-mounted dish and she picked it up, sniffing appreciatively at the spicy aroma she instantly recognised as the one which always clung to Aaron Blake's skin. She held the soap under the jets of warm water then lathered her hands and ran them up and down the delicate curves of her body as she soaped her skin. The heady musky scent seemed to envelop her, stirring her senses, and she shivered suddenly despite the heat.

It seemed such an intimate thing to do, to use this soap and share this heady perfume with him. It awakened feelings inside her she didn't want to feel ... ever!

Aaron Blake was her friend, the Good Samaritan who had stopped to help the traveller fallen by the roadside. She didn't want to imagine them sharing any sort of intimacies. Something told her she couldn't cope with that.

Setting the soap back in the dish, she rinsed the fragrant lather from her skin, letting the hot water pound endlessly over her flesh and wash away every tiny trace of the perfume. Tears welled to her eyes and she turned her face up to the spray to wash them away too, but more kept on coming, mingling saltily with the clear, fresh water.

Last night she had cried for her past, for old hurts, old wounds and things that she'd lost, but now she cried for her future and all the things she could never have. Somehow, this was far more painful.

CHAPTER FIVE

AARON BLAKE was just coming out of the sitting-room when Kate came downstairs. He waited in the hall for her, his gaze lingering on the red puffiness beneath her eyes which no amount of make-up could disguise, but he said nothing. Kate came to a halt beside him, pushing a damp curl of fine red hair off her cheek, feeling suddenly nervous in his company.

'So, how did you sleep, Kate? You didn't spend the whole night lying awake worrying about your sister, I hope.'

'No. I slept very well, thank you. I . . . I'm really sorry about before, barging in on you like that. It just never occurred to me that you'd be using the bathroom.'

He shrugged, his big shoulders moving easily under the light blue cashmere sweater, and for a brief moment Kate remembered how those shoulders had looked, gleaming hard and golden in the light, before she hurriedly clamped down on the memory.

'Oh, don't mention it. I'm only sorry I gave you such a shock, that's all. It's been a while since I've had anyone staying here overnight so I never even thought about locking the connecting door. Mind you, I doubt if I'll bother doing it again if that's the sort of treat I can look forward to. That little outfit you were wearing was very fetching, Kate.'

There was a teasing lightness to his words but Kate couldn't help the sudden surge of colour which stained her cheeks a brilliant carmine. She wasn't used to being teased like that and didn't know how to respond to it. Maybe if she'd been more experienced she would have been able to make some light, casual remark, but her only real experience with men had been with Jonathan, and that had been too brief to teach her anything about sophisticated banter. Now just the thought of how much he had seen of her slender body in those wispy bits of lace and satin held her tongue-tied.

'Do you know that it's almost a pleasure to tease you, Kate, just to see how you blush.' He smiled at her, a strange intentness in his eyes as he studied her hot face. 'Can you really be so sweetly innocent, I ask myself?'

The question was light enough yet Kate felt suddenly uncomfortable. She looked away, smoothing her hands over her skirt, feeling sick. Was she innocent? After all she'd gone through during the trial could she really consider herself to be that? Would *he* think she was innocent if he found out about her past? She didn't know, couldn't hazard a guess as to what his reaction might be, but suddenly the thought of just how quickly those blue eyes might fill with contempt made her want to find some deep dark hole to hide in.

'Have I said something wrong?'

Aaron leant a shoulder against the wall as he stared thoughtfully at her, and hurriedly Kate pulled herself together. She didn't want him getting curious about her, didn't want him asking questions she couldn't answer. In a few hours she and this man would part company forever and for some reason it seemed important that he should continue to think well of her.

'No, of course you haven't. I was just worrying about Chrissie, that's all. Would you mind if I rang the hospital to find out how she is?'

When had she learned to lie so easily and with such conviction? Kate didn't know, but it wasn't an accomplishment she was proud of even though it served her well.

'Of course not. Let me get the number for you.'

He pulled a directory off the shelf next to the telephone and thumbed through it, picking up a pen to circle the number before handing it to her.

'Here you are. I'll go and pour that coffee I promised you while you make the call. And don't worry. I'm sure your sister will be fine.'

He smiled reassuringly at her and Kate nodded, waiting until he had disappeared along the passage leading to the rear of the house before dialling the number. She was connected almost immediately to the ward sister on Chrissie's floor who briefly informed her that Mrs Knight was quite comfortable. Kate thanked the woman and hung up, resting her hand against the receiver as she wondered what she should do next. Obviously she would go and visit Chrissie again this morning, just to check for herself that she was indeed on the mend, but after that what should she do and where should she go? She couldn't impose on Aaron's hospitality any longer, nor could she go to the flat and stay with Jack. He had quite enough on his mind right now without being landed with an uninvited guest. Suddenly the day stretched before her both empty and lonely, and she gave a weary little sigh.

'What's wrong? Not bad news, I hope.'

Aaron came up quietly behind her and Kate swung round startled.

'Er...no...no. Chrissie is fine. She spent a comfortable night according to the ward sister.'

'Then why so sad? You look as if you've lost the proverbial pound and not even found the penny. What's troubling you, Kate?'

There it was again, that same intentness in the blue gaze he levelled at her, the same nuance in his deep voice, yet what had caused it? Kate didn't know, but frankly she already had enough on her mind to worry about without adding that to the pile! She shrugged, looking down at her fingers which were nervously twisting the hem of her jumper, wondering what to say. She really didn't want to tell him what was the matter. He might feel obliged to ask her to stay, and she didn't want that, didn't want to feel like an object of his pity. She still had some pride left at least.

'Nothing,' she mumbled at last. 'Now how about that coffee you promised? I could do with a cup to wake me up properly.'

She went to walk past him but he caught her arm, his long fingers holding her firmly.

'Don't give me that, sweetheart. Let's face it, you were wide awake the very minute you set eyes on me in the bathroom this morning, so I doubt if you need a cup of coffee that much! Now we can stay here as long as you like, Kate, but one way or another you're going to tell me what's wrong!'

Just who did he think he was, keeping her here and giving her orders like her lord and master? Kate rounded on him, her green eyes flashing with annoyance.

'Let me go! If I don't choose to tell you what's wrong then that's my business, not yours!' She wrenched her arm free and marched back towards the stairs. 'I'm fetching my coat because I have no intention of staying here in this house a moment longer and listening to you issuing orders!'

'And where will you go?'

'What do you mean, where will I go? To the hospital, of course.' She refused to look at him, ripples of anger coursing hotly through her body. She was tired of being pushed around and told what to do and when to do it. For months now she'd had to put up with all that from Tony, but she didn't have to put up with it from this man!

'And after that?'

His voice was calm, unhurried, and reluctantly she shot him a quick glance. He was leaning against the wall again, his hands pushed deep into the pockets of his grey trousers, a lock of dark hair falling rakishly over his wide brow, and he looked so at ease that she could have wept. Obviously what she'd just said had meant nothing to him. She might have well saved her breath!

He smiled coolly at her, his eyes very dark against the light golden tan of his skin. 'How much money have you got in your purse, Kate?' he asked calmly, watching the rapid play of emotions on her face. 'Enough to pay for a hotel room? London is a very expensive place to stay, in case you've forgotten.'

'Of course I haven't forgotten,' she snapped, stung by the truth of his words. 'But it's my business what I do and how I manage, isn't it?'

He shook his head, straightening away from the wall, his face suddenly grim. 'No, it isn't. I brought you here, Kate, and it's my duty to make certain that nothing happens to you whether you like it or not. Face it, love, you can't go bothering your sister or her husband at present, can you? They have enough on their plates right now.'

He was right, of course, his words only mirroring her own recent thoughts. There was no way she could trouble either Chrissie or Jack with her problems right now. They had to concentrate on their own lives and on getting Chrissie well again. The realisation made her feel more alone than ever.

'So what do you suggest?' she asked quietly, her shoulders slumping in dejection.

He shrugged. 'I don't know yet, but I'm sure we can come up with something. Now come and get that coffee before it goes cold. As it's about the one and only thing I make which tastes even halfway decent it seems a shame to miss out on the chance.'

He held his hand out and Kate came slowly down the stairs again and slid her fingers into his.

'It will be all right in the end, Kate, you'll see.'

Will it? she wanted to ask, but somehow couldn't put a voice to her fears so that the words were silent, the question unspoken, echoing round and round in her head as she went with him along the hall. Would everything really be all right? Would all her problems disappear and life turn out to be something other than a struggle against the odds? She wished she could believe it, but deep down she had the strangest feeling that her association with this man would only lead to trouble!

The hospital was bustling with activity when Kate arrived. Aaron dropped her off at the gates leading to the main driveway, making her promise to ring him when she wanted to leave again. He was adamant that he wanted to come and collect her, and somehow Kate didn't have the strength or the heart to argue with him. It was a strange feeling to be cosseted and cared for this way, one she had never experienced before even when she'd been dating Jonathan. He had been quite happy to let her make her own way home even late at night, and at the time Kate had never questioned the fact. She had been so much in love with him that she'd been blind to all the tell-tale signs which another woman might have interpreted correctly as a lack of real concern for her welfare. Now, however, it brought home to her even more forcibly just how little Jonathan Knight had really cared for her. She had just been a useful tool in his desire for wealth.

The bitter taste of the thought stayed with her as she raced through the rain along the drive and in through the hospital doors. She paused for a moment, brushing raindrops off her coat and flicking her fingers through her hair to separate the damp strands while she composed herself again. She didn't want Chrissie sensing she was unhappy and worrying about her. She had done everything she possibly could to help Kate over the past painful year and now it was Kate's turn to help her. So, if she had to pin on a happy face and smile and laugh while inside she was aching, she would do it.

Kate made her way along the maze of corridors and up the stairs, taking the route Aaron had taken the previous night and vaguely wishing he were there with her again. He had been such a comfort to her yesterday, his calmness and strength a rock against her fears. The trouble was it would be only too easy to slip into the habit of relying on him, of letting him take over her life and make all the decisions, but she couldn't do that. He had done so much for her already. There was no way she could ever really pay him back.

Chrissie was sitting propped against a mound of pillows when Kate walked into her room and, despite the fact that she was a trifle pale, she looked just as beautiful as ever, the soft, fluffy blue bedjacket draped round her shoulders emphasising her golden colouring. She held her hands out to Kate, smiling in delight to see her.

'Kate! Oh, it's lovely to see you. I know you were here last night but I was still so woozy from the fall that I didn't really know what was going on. But it's such a long way to come! Jack should never have phoned you!'

'Of course he should, and don't you dare give that poor man a hard time about phoning me. He was absolutely distraught yesterday. You scared the life out of him, Chrissie, and me too for that matter.'

Pressing a kiss to her sister's cheek, Kate sat down next to the bed, looking sternly at her.

Chrissie sighed. 'Yes, I know, and believe me Jack has already torn me off a strip about it this morning now that the shock has worn off a bit. I'm sorry, Kate. I know it was a stupid thing to do, but I just wanted to get the curtains hung to finish off the nursery. I never thought that the ladder would slip like that.'

'Ladder! You were up a ladder in your condition!' Wide-eyed with horror, Kate stared down at the rounded swell of Chrissie's stomach before glaring at her. 'I don't know about tearing you off a strip, I think Jack should keep you under lock and key if that's the sort of crazy thing you do.'

Chrissie wriggled uncomfortably, looking down at her slender fingers as she twisted the narrow band of diamonds and sapphires Jack had given her when they had married. 'I know, I know, and I promise I won't do it ever again. This baby is far too precious, Kate, and I wouldn't want to harm it. It was just an impulse. You know what I'm like; I have to get things done there and then and can't bear to wait.'

'I know, but you're going to have to, at least for the next couple of months.'

'All right, don't nag. I have the feeling that Jack's going to do enough of that for both of you in the next couple of months! Now what's all this he's been telling me about some man flying you down here in his private plane? What did he say his name was . . . Aaron something? Who is he, Kate, and how long have you known him?'

Neatly turning the conversation around, Chrissie sat up straighter against the pillows and pinned Kate with her best big-sister stare, and hastily Kate tried to work out an edited version of how she and Aaron Blake had met. After all, if she told Chrissie the true fact that she'd only met him a few days ago then she would most probably throw a fit. Which girl in her right mind would go off with a man she scarcely knew and then stay the night in his house? Choosing her words with extreme caution, Kate filled her in on the facts as best she could.

'His name is Aaron Blake and I met him in Liverpool where he's involved in some sort of dockland regeneration project.'

'I see. And how old is he, where does he live and is he married?'

Kate filtered that set of questions through her brain realising with a start that she could only truthfully answer one of them. She knew where he lived all right, but as to his age or even his marital status she had no idea. Suddenly the idea that Aaron Blake might be married was painful.

'Come on, then, Kate, give. You do know something about his background, don't you?'

There was concern in the look Chrissie shot at her and Kate hurriedly pulled herself together. She didn't want Chrissie worrying about her.

'Of course I do, silly. He lives here in London actually. You should see his house, Chrissie. It's really lovely. Of course, he has a housekeeper to keep every-thing in perfect order.'

'Well, thank heavens for that! I was none too pleased with Jack when he told me he'd let you stay the night there. Oh, I know he said that this Mr Blake seemed a pleasant enough man, but you can never tell, can y——Jack!' She broke off abruptly as Jack came quietly into the room and Kate breathed a silent sigh of relief at the interruption. The Spanish Inquisition had nothing on Chrissie when she was extracting information!

She turned to smile at her brother-in-law, her eyes misting slightly as she saw the expression on his face as he looked at Chrissie. It must be wonderful to be loved like that, she thought wistfully, watching as he bent to kiss his wife's cheek then take her hand tenderly in his. It was obvious that they both had eyes for no one else at that moment and Kate felt suddenly incredibly lonely. She stood up, not wanting to intrude on them when they had so much to talk about, so many plans to make for their future and their baby.

'Don't let me chase you away, Kate,' Jack said, turning to smile at her, his fingers still linked with Chrissie's. 'Stay a bit longer.'

'I've stayed quite long enough. I'm sure you both have lots to talk about, but I'll come back tonight if they're going to keep you in a bit longer, Chrissie.'

'Unfortunately yes. The doctor has insisted that I stay here in bed for the next few days while they keep me under observation. Just a precaution, you know,' she added quickly as she saw the fleeting alarm which crossed her husband's face. 'They are ninety-nine per cent certain that there's been no damage done, but I suppose I'll have to go along with it.'

'You most definitely will. You took quite a fall, lady, and don't you forget it.'

Jack's voice was unusually stern, but the glance he shot at his beautiful wife was anything but that and Kate grinned. They were such a good match for each other, her impetuous, volatile sister and this tall, strong man. If nothing else good had come out of last year's fiasco at least this had happened. If Chrissie hadn't gone to Jack's casino, determined to prove to the world that Kate was innocent, then they would never have met. This was the real gleaming silver lining at the very heart of the dark cloud.

'You talk some sense into her, Jack,' Kate said with a loving smile at them both. 'I'll see you tonight, then, I expect.'

She turned to go, pausing as Jack called to her.

'Oh, Kate, I almost forgot. Aaron Blake is waiting outside the gates for you. I saw him on the way in and he asked me to tell you. I had the idea that he didn't trust you to call him when you were leaving in case you thought you were bothering him.'

'Mmm, sounds as if Mr Blake already has a good idea just how mule-headed our Katie can be, doesn't it?' Chrissie teased, determined to get her own back for Kate's unaccustomed bossiness.

'I'm quite sure Blake has Kate summed up all right. From what I've heard of the man he's a sharp operator, one of the shrewdest businessmen in the country. He started off with nothing and rumour has it that he's fought his way to the top by sheer grit and determination. Actually I was rather surprised when I finally realised just who he was, Kate. He's not known for his generosity, so how come he went out of his way to help you?' Jack sat down on the side of the bed and slid an arm round his wife to pull her head gently against his shoulder.

For a moment Kate hesitated, wondering what she could say when she didn't even know the answer to that question herself. Why *had* Aaron Blake helped her so readily? From what Jack had said it seemed to be way out of character for him to do such a thing.

'You're not in any kind of trouble, are you, Kate? This Aaron Blake hasn't...well, he hasn't got any kind of hold over you, has he?'

Genuine concern lit Chrissie's face and hastily Kate forced herself to speak. The very last thing she wanted was for Chrissie to start worrying about her.

'No, of course he hasn't. Don't be silly, Chrissie. You're letting your imagination run away with you! I probably caught him at a weak moment yesterday, then, seeing as Jack almost press-ganged him into letting me spend the night at his house, what could he say?'

'Jack, you didn't! Why, that was a dreadful thing to do! How could you...?'

Kate grinned, shooting a wicked, mocking glance at Jack as she crept from the room. From the look of things he was going to have some fast talking to do to get out of that one! Still, he deserved it. If he hadn't asked about Aaron Blake's reasons for helping her then Chrissie would never have thought anything about it. Mind you, in all honesty she could understand what was worrying Jack about the situation. Why had he done it . . . why?

Her footsteps slowed as she stepped out into the rain and made her way slowly down the driveway towards the waiting car. The time had come to make Aaron Blake explain, give her answers to all the questions which were whirling round and round in her head, yet deep down Kate had the uncomfortable feeling that she might not like what he told her.

Aaron had the door open even before she reached the car and Kate slid hurriedly inside, murmuring an apology as her wet coat made damp patches on the pale soft leather seat.

'Don't worry. It will soon dry. You're absolutely soaked, Kate! Come on, let's get you back before you catch a chill.'

He smiled at her, then turned the key in the ignition to start the car with a well-heeled roar, but Kate caught hold of his arm before he could set it into gear.

'Wait just a minute, Aaron, please.'

He flicked a quick glance at her, his eyes very clear and bright in the dim confines of the car, and Kate had the strangest feeling that he was looking deep into her mind and reading every single one of her thoughts. She glanced down, staring at her hand resting so palely on the dark sleeve of his wool jacket, then slowly withdrew it and let it fall to her lap.

'What is it, Kate?' he asked quietly, so quietly that she had to strain to hear the words over the drumming of the rain on the metal roof and the muted throb of the engine.

'It's just that...that...' She floundered, wondering how best to phrase the next sentence and make him understand why she needed answers to her questions.

'Yes, Kate?'

There was authority in the deep voice now, a touch of steel, and Kate swallowed hard, realising she was in danger of making a mess of it all if she wasn't careful.

'I just wanted to thank you, for all this.' She waved a hand round, silently indicating the rain-soaked street and the comfortable luxury of the car sheltering her from the elements. 'I really appreciate what you've done for me, Aaron.'

'But?' he prompted, and Kate shivered as she heard the harsh note in his voice. At that moment he seemed a million miles away from the kind stranger who had dropped everything to help her. Kate would have given anything to turn back the clock, forget about her questions and his answers, but she couldn't. She had to go on.

She looked up, forcing herself to meet the cold blue eyes which were regarding her so closely. 'But I really think it's time we had a talk, you and I. You've been very kind to me and I'm truly grateful, but I can't keep imposing on you like this.'

'Have I ever given you reason to think I consider it to be an imposition, Kate?'

Kate shrugged, suddenly wary of the anger growing in his eyes. She didn't want to make him angry, but she had to set the record straight.

'No, of course you haven't. You've been more than kind, but I can't keep accepting things off you, Aaron. There's no way I can ever pay you back.'

'I don't expect you to pay me back, as you put it, Kate.' He stared out of the windscreen, his face in profile looking harshly unfamiliar. 'Ask anyone who knows me and they'll soon tell you that I never do anything I don't want to do. I chose to help you and that's it as far as I'm concerned. There is no debt to repay, not now, not ever.'

'But don't you see, that's just what I can't under-stand about all this,' she cried, turning in her seat to face him. 'Why did you help me? Why did you go out of your way like that? You could have done what anyone else would have, made a few comforting noises then turned your back on me and left me to sort out my own problems!' She pushed the strands of hair falling softly against her cheek behind her ears with hands which suddenly trembled. 'Just what do you get out of all this, Aaron Blake? I wish I could believe that you'd done it for some sort of altruistic reason but, frankly, I gave up believing in fairy-tales years ago! What do you stand to gain?'

'Nothing apart from a whole load of aggravation from the look of it. Look, Kate, what do you expect me to say? That it was love at first sight? That I saw you in that café and fell for you? I'm afraid I don't go in for that sort of thing even if you do, sweetheart. I was there, you needed help and I took pity on you. That's it, in a nutshell, so let's end this ridiculous conversation, shall we, and get back? I have a pile of work to do which is far more important than sitting here discussing your overactive imagination!'

He gunned the engine then slid the car into gear, obviously thinking he'd had the last word—but he was wrong! There was no way Kate was going anywhere with him after what he'd just said—no way she was going to be a recipient of any more of his charity. Pity! Damn him to hell for saying that, for having the gall to pity her!

'I'm not going anywhere with you, Mr Blake,' she said coldly, her voice splintered with ice. 'I might not have much in this world but I do have my self-respect. I don't need charity or hand-outs from you or anyone!'

'Kate, you've got this all wrong. Look, I'm sorry. Maybe I was a bit rough on you——'

'Rough! No, you weren't rough, you were rude, downright rude, but no matter.' She opened her bag and scrabbled in her purse to pull out a ten-pound note and a handful of silver, dropping it on to the dashboard, uncaring that several of the coins fell to the floor. 'Here, this should cover a night's board and lodgings. I'll let you have a cheque for the cost of the flight down just as soon as I can. Goodbye, Mr Blake. I can't actually say it's been a pleasure meeting you, but it has been an experience—one I hope I shall never have to repeat!'

She wrenched the car door open and jumped out, hurrying down the street, weaving a path between the traffic with scant regard for her safety. Behind her she could hear Aaron calling her name, his voice hoarse with fury, but she didn't look back, didn't even glance

over her shoulder. She didn't want to see him ever
again, didn't want to be reminded of what he'd said,
how he'd mocked her with his cruel words. The very
last thing she had wanted from that man was
pity...damn him!

CHAPTER SIX

NIGHT was drawing in, settling grey shadows along the city streets. Kate rounded the last corner, her footsteps slowing as she saw the sign gleaming against the night sky. She hadn't wanted to come, hadn't wanted to test herself against the bitter pain of memory today of all days, yet what else could she have done? With little or no cash left in her purse where else could she stay the night except at Jack's and Chrissie's flat above the casino?

She walked slowly on, pausing outside the elegant building, her eyes skimming over its imposing façade. It was an hour or so before it was due to open and, apart from the gleaming sign of a knight in armour, the whole place was in darkness, yet suddenly Kate could see it as it had looked that first time she'd been there, when Jonathan had brought her. She could still remember how she'd felt that night, standing on the steps, her heart racing and the blood pounding wildly round her veins. She had been so excited, so impressed both by Jonathan and the glamour of his job running one of London's top nightspots. The whole night had been magical, made even more so by the fact that she had been falling in love with her handsome escort and had believed that he had felt the same about her.

Closing her eyes, oblivious to the stinging rain-drops hitting her skin, Kate gave herself up to the memories, yet the strange thing was it seemed impossible to conjure up an image of Jonathan. His face was shadowed, flickering, wavering, without flesh or substance, and in a flash it came to Kate that Jonathan was no more real now than he had been then. Everything about him had been false right from the beginning. He had lied and deceived her, used her, then turned his back on her when she was in trouble. The man she had thought him to be, the man she had loved so desperately, just didn't exist.

The thought brought her abruptly back to the present and Kate opened her eyes, her face colouring as she saw the strange looks she was getting from passers-by. Pulling the collar of her coat tighter round her neck, she hurried past the casino and down a narrow passage which led to the rear of the building and the entrance to the flat, her heart sinking when she found that was in total darkness also. Where on earth was Jack? Had he gone to the hospital again, or what?

With a weary sigh, Kate huddled against the gates to the courtyard, praying that Jack would put in an appearance soon. She was so wet from the hours she'd spent tramping the streets all afternoon that she had the nasty feeling it wasn't only her shoes which were squelching but her skin! For a moment her mind flicked back to where she'd spent the previous night, to Aaron's house and all the quiet luxury of the room he'd given her, before she hastily brought it back under control. She wouldn't let herself think about that man again, wouldn't let herself remember what he'd said to her. She didn't want anyone to pity her ever again!

Time passed slowly and Kate kept glancing at her watch to check up on the creeping progress of the minute hand until the fading light made even that piece of entertainment impossible. The passageway was very dark, the faint glow from a distant street lamp too pale to light the inky shadows, and gradually Kate began to feel uneasy. She glanced nervously round, her eyes sweeping over the dark patches, the murky shadows, wondering what was causing the feeling. She hadn't heard anyone come down the passageway while she'd been there, but with the noise of the rain beating against the rooftops it was just possible that she could have missed hearing any footsteps. Was there someone there, standing in those shadows, watching her?

Slowly and methodically she checked the alley out, her heart bumping painfully as her eyes fell on a deep patch of shadow some yards away. Had something moved just then, a shifting of the darkness, a rearranging of the inky patterns?

For a long minute Kate stared at the spot, but it was impossible to tell if she'd imagined it without going closer, and she had no intention of doing that! If there was someone there then he or she could stay there and good luck to them. She had no intention of keeping them company a moment longer. She would go round to the front of the casino and see if Jack was there. If he wasn't, then she would see if anyone could let her into the flat to wait for him. It was what any sensible person would have done a good half-hour ago. Her brain must be as soggy as the rest of her!

As fast as her numb legs would allow she hurried back down the alley, pausing for a moment as she reached the corner to glance back over her shoulder. The glow from the street lamp shone on her hair, turning the damp strands to a brilliant burnished copper. A stone rattled across the alley and Kate jumped, searching the shadows with wide, startled eyes, but she could see no sign of anyone following her. Heaven alone knew who was there or what they wanted, but there was no way she was going to hang round and find out!

She took to her heels and raced round to the front of the building, almost flinging herself through the doors to the casino in her haste to get away from the unseen, menacing presence. Light flared in her eyes, blinding her, and she blinked rapidly to clear her vision, then felt herself go hot with embarrassment when she saw what a stir her sudden appearance had caused.

Beautifully gowned women and elegantly dressed men were standing in the huge hallway openly staring at her, and for a moment Kate seriously considered turning tail and retreating! It was only the thought of what might be waiting outside which made her stay and brazen it out.

She walked across to the reception desk, vividly aware of the nasty squelch of water in her sodden shoes, and forced a smile to her stiff lips.

'Is Mr Knight available, please?'

The receptionist did her best, Kate had to admit it, but even she couldn't stop the astonishment which crossed her face at the sight of such a dishevelled figure asking for her employer.

'Er ... er ... no. I'm sorry, but Mr Knight isn't here tonight. Can I help you?'

There was a trace of distaste on the girl's beautiful face now as she skimmed a glance over Kate's sodden clothing, and Kate felt a sudden wave of anger rise inside her.

'Perhaps you can,' she answered with a touch of hauteur quite ruined by the sudden shiver which racked her body and made her voice quiver. 'I am Mr Knight's sister-in-law. Is there any way that you can let me into his flat to wait for him?'

'Well, I don't know.'

Obviously nonplussed, the girl glanced round, then beckoned to a heavy-set man standing to one side of the entrance to the casino. She whispered something to him, her glance skimming back to where Kate stood dripping puddles all over the beautiful Persian carpet, and instinctively Kate stood up straighter. The man shot her a quick glance, his eyes openly assessing, then shook his head and Kate knew as clear as anything what would happen next.

The receptionist turned back to her, her face set into a practised smile which didn't quite reach her eyes.

'I'm sorry, but I'm afraid that won't be possible. Mr and Mrs Knight are the only ones who have keys to the flat and with neither of them here tonight I can't help you.'

She stared pointedly at Kate, then glanced at the door, obviously expecting her to accept the rebuff and leave, but Kate knew she wasn't going to give up without a fight. She was tired of being treated like dirt, like nothing!

'If you can't help me then find me someone who can,' she ordered. 'I am not leaving here until I talk to someone in authority.'

Her voice rang round the quiet hallway and out of the corner of her eyes she saw the man take a step towards her, a hint of menace in the gesture. It was obvious that he was going to throw her out and she turned to face him, her body stiffening in readiness.

'Kate? Is that really you, lassie?'

Kate spun round, searching the crowd for the owner of the familiar voice, and felt her knees go weak with relief as she spotted him pushing his way through the throng.

'Mac! Oh, thank heavens you're here.' She clasped his hand, smiling delightedly at the elderly man who was in charge of the stage lighting for the casino's famous cabaret, and one of Chrissie and Jack's dearest friends. 'I need somewhere to stay for the night. Can you let me into the flat?'

'I wish I could, but I've not got a key, lassie.' He nodded towards the man who had halted a few yards away. 'That's OK, Frank. I'll take care of Miss Warren now. Come along, Kate.'

Taking her arm, he led her across the hall, his lined face creased with worry as he felt the heavy shiver which shook her body. 'I don't know what you've been up to, young lady, but if Chrissie saw you she'd have a fit and that's the truth. Now come along in here and get that wet coat off.'

He led her briskly into one of the small dressing-rooms, flicking on the electric fire before looking sternly at her. Kate smiled shakily at him, her hands trembling so much that she could barely ease the buttons free from the sodden fabric. Dropping the coat on to the floor, she knelt before the fire, holding her hands out to the warmth.

'Now listen, Kate, do you want me to phone the hospital and see if Jack is there? I've not seen him all afternoon, but he's bound to go there some time.'

'Would you, please? Thanks, Mac. I had planned on going myself, but I don't think it would be a good idea right now, not in this state. Chrissie would only start to worry about what had been going on. If you'll just leave a message that I've been delayed, then I can wait here till Jack gets back and dry off a bit. I'll be fine, honestly. It's just so good to be out of all that rain at last.'

Mac looked worried as he studied her dishevelled appearance and absolute pallor. 'Frankly, you look as if you should be tucked up in bed with a hot toddy, but there's not much I can do about it right now.' He glanced at his watch. 'Now listen, it's nearly time for the first cabaret to start so I'll have to leave you. Stay here and dry off, and don't leave! Or Jack will have my guts for garters.'

'I won't, I promise. And thanks, Mac. I don't know what I would have done if you hadn't appeared. I was getting nowhere with that receptionist.'

'Can you blame her? You look more like something from the lost and found than the boss's sister-in-law! Anyhow, I'll see you later.'

With a final worried smile he left, closing the door quietly behind him, and Kate let her head droop wearily against the side of a nearby chair. She knew she should get out of the wet clothes and find something dry to wear, but somehow it seemed to demand more effort than she could manage. She would just rest for a while and then, when she felt a bit stronger, do something about tidying herself up. She didn't want Jack to see her in this deplorable state; he had quite enough to worry about with Chrissie.

She slid down on to the floor, pillowing her head on her arms, feeling the shivers racing up and down her body. The fire was turned on to full power but it seemed to be making very little difference to the cold which cramped her limbs. Curling into a tight ball, Kate tried to retain as much heat as she could, but it seemed an unequal struggle. She was just so tired, worn out by the day and all that had happened. All she really wanted to do at that moment was sleep.

She closed her eyes, nestling her head deeper into the crook of her arm, and let her mind drift. Images of the day began to flicker inside her closed lids, moving pictures without sound or sequence, reminders of all that had happened, and she stirred restlessly on the carpet covering the floor. It had been such a horrible day and she didn't want to remember even half of it, yet she wasn't proof against the sudden rush of memories.

Then slowly, as she lay there, a face rose up in her mind, a strong face with clearly defined features and eyes like sapphires, and involuntarily her lips moved to form his name.

'Aaron,' she whispered. 'Oh, Aaron!'

Hours before she had run from him in anger, yet now, strangely, just the sound of his name and the memory of his face seemed to offer comfort, and she slept.

'Kate! Kate, can you hear me? Wake up.'

The voice cut into her sleep, forcing back the delicious dreams, and Kate moved reluctantly.

'Come on, Kate. Wake up! You can't stay there all night.'

A hand gripped her shoulder and shook her roughly, and with a tiny murmur Kate forced her heavy lids open. For a hazy second she stared up into the face so close to hers, then smiled as she reached up and ran a gentle finger down the lean cheek.

'Mmm . . . I was just dreaming about you,' she said sleepily, her voice warm and faintly husky. 'Such a lovely dr——Aaron! I . . . What are you doing here?'

She shot upright, groaning as her cold, cramped muscles screamed in protest at the sudden movement. Pushing her hair from her face, she glanced round the room, letting her mind wake fully to the realisation of where she was and just who was with her. Slowly, her gaze slid back to the tall figure towering over her and travelled up the long length of a pair of dark-clad legs, over a solidly muscled torso to his face, and she felt her cheeks fill with colour.

She staggered to her feet, flinching as Aaron Blake caught her arm to steady her. She pulled away and stepped back a pace, the memory of their last meeting still too vividly clear to let her feel comfortable in his presence.

Anger flared inside her, then swiftly faded as she remembered her dreams, and the way she had reached out to touch his cheek that way. How could she have done that? Now her only hope for salvaging her pride was to act as coolly and rationally as she could. The trouble was she had never felt less cool or rational in the whole of her life faced with the flesh-and-blood version of the man who had just filled her dreams in such a shockingly intimate way!

'You look dreadful, Kate. What the hell have you been doing with yourself?'

The harsh observation was just what she needed to whip her reeling senses back into shape. Kate stood up straighter, her eyes frosty as she faced him squarely. Just who did he think he was, telling her that she looked awful and then demanding to know what she'd been doing? Why, anyone would think he owned her from the way he spoke.

'Never mind what I've been doing, what are you doing here? Did you follow me?'

She glared at him, her pulse leaping as she noticed the flicker of anger which crossed his face at her words. It wasn't hard to imagine that Aaron Blake could be a powerful opponent if he chose to be, so was it really wise to antagonise him like this when they were alone? The sensible thing to do would be to smooth things over, but looking at his grim face

Kate knew she wasn't going to be sensible . . . not yet! Some tiny inner demon was whispering to her, goading her into speaking her mind and to hell with the consequences. It was a dangerous game and one Kate suddenly knew she wanted to play!

'Well?' she demanded. 'Not lost for an answer, are you, Mr Blake? Not too shy to admit that you like playing detective and following women?'

'For your information, I didn't follow you. No one but a maniac could have followed you the way you were going, weaving your way through the traffic like that! Jack phoned and asked me to come, if you really want to know.'

'I don't believe you. Why on earth should Jack phone you? What have you got to do with any of this? Oh, I'm grateful to you for flying me down here, but that's it, as far as it goes. None of this has anything at all to do with you, so why don't you get out of here and leave me in peace? I don't need your help any longer, thank you very much, so why not go and find some other poor damsel to rescue, if that's how you get your kicks?'

Why had she said that, thrown all his kindness back at him in such a fashion? For a moment Kate stood rigid, appalled that she could have said such a thing, then took a hasty step backwards as he came towards her. His blue eyes were glittering, tiny flames flickering angrily in their depths as he glared down at her and, for the first time since she'd met him, Kate really felt afraid. She spun round, heading for the door, but he was too quick for her.

He caught her shoulder, his long, hard fingers biting deep into the bone as he hauled her against him.

'So the little kitten has claws, has she? I always had the feeling there was more to you than met the eye, Kate, that behind that sweetly innocent façade lay true steel. You'd never have got this far without it!'

'I don't know what you mean. Let me go, Aaron! You're hurting me!'

She wriggled round, twisting desperately in an attempt to get free, but although he loosened his hold a fraction he didn't let her go, just drew her closer against the hard length of his body.

'Let you go... oh, no, not yet. Not until I've had my reward.'

'Reward? What reward? Stop talking in riddles.'

Kate glared at him, feeling the blood racing hotly through her veins as she saw the way he was looking at her, saw as clearly as if it had been written in foot-high letters the intention on his face. Suddenly the air around them seemed to be filled with tension so thick that Kate felt breathless through lack of oxygen. She had done this, deliberately provoked him and fanned the flames of his anger until they burned almost out of control. Now her whole body went tense with expectancy of what must follow.

'My reward for flying you down here, of course. You've been expecting it, haven't you, Kate? Been wondering how and when I would demand my payment, so wonder no more!'

He bent his head and Kate felt her heart stop, then leap in crazy little jerks and bounces as his mouth closed over hers in a harsh kiss which held no trace of gentleness, no hint of concession. His lips were hard, demanding, provoking a response which she was suddenly powerless to resist. With a tiny moan, Kate pressed herself closer, opening her mouth so that he could deepen the kiss, feeling the heavy shudder which shook him with a swift flare of triumph.

Despite all he had said to her that morning it wasn't pity he was feeling now, not by a long chalk! He wanted her. She could feel it in the demands his lips were making, in the way his tongue plundered the sweetness of her mouth with a hot desperation, in the way his body trembled against hers. Oh, he might be angry with her, but it wasn't anger which gave the kiss such magic, wasn't anger which fuelled this sudden burning passion. He wanted her! And she wanted him too. It was what she had been aware of from the beginning, what she'd been afraid of, but now Kate was too caught up in the moment to really feel afraid. It was as though her life had stopped and started with this moment . . . with this kiss.

The kiss ran on and on, a glorious blaze of sensation, burning away the anger, the hurt, the pain. Cleansed of all those emotions, all Kate could think of was the man who was holding her, his lips demanding yet giving so much. Then, slowly, he eased his mouth away and Kate opened her eyes to stare into his face, all the wonder and magic she had felt shining softly in her eyes.

He smiled at her, brushing a light kiss up the curve of her flushed cheek, his face unexpectedly tender so that for a moment Kate felt her breath catch tight in her throat. She reached up to run a finger gently across his lips, scarcely able to believe that anything so magical could be real, then felt her pulse race as he nipped it gently with his teeth.

'Well, Kate, as rewards go that was definitely worth having. Better than any amount of money, in fact!'

His tone was deliberately light and teasing, and Kate realised with a sudden rush of gratitude that he was giving her time to gather her wits about her again. She must look as shaken by that kiss as she felt, lord help her!

She moved away, putting a few feet between them before she answered, trying to keep her voice as light as his had been.

'I'm glad you think so. Every gallant knight should be amply rewarded for his efforts, don't you think?'

'I most certainly do. Look, Kate, about this morning and what I said to you, I——'

She didn't want to hear what he had to say, didn't want him to repeat the reason why he had helped her. She didn't want his pity, especially not now, with the memory of that kiss still warming her lips.

'No! Please don't say anything, Aaron. This morning is best——'

'It was a lie, Kate, a huge great lie,' he said abruptly, stepping forwards to catch hold of her hands. He lifted them to his lips, kissing first one then the other, and Kate had to hold herself rigid to control the shudder which raced through her body. She looked down, terrified of what he might read in her eyes at that moment, terrified of how vulnerable it made her.

'This morning I was angry, Kate. I'm not used to having people cross-question me or demand explanations for my actions. I reacted instinctively, saying the first thing which came into my head, and I'm sorry.'

He sounded sincere but Kate pulled away, needing to put some distance between them so that she could think.

'Will you forgive me, Kate, please? The last thing I feel for you is pity, or anything else like that. That's part of the trouble.'

There was a strange note in his deep voice and Kate studied him thoughtfully, wondering what had caused it, but there was little she could tell from his expression. Why was it that, instead of making everything clearer between them, each time he spoke it made things seem even more mysterious, as though there was something he was hiding from her? Surely the time had come for her to expect some answers.

'I accept your apology, Aaron,' she said quietly, 'but if it wasn't pity, as you say, why did you help me?'

He seemed to hesitate, as though he was fighting some hard inner battle, then shrugged. 'I can't tell you right now, Kate. I know it's hard for you, but will you accept the fact that I don't mean to cause you any harm and trust me just for a few days longer? Lord knows I never want to go through another episode like this morning! I was terrified that you were going to get yourself killed running off through the traffic like that.'

'Is that why you didn't chase me?'

'Partly, and partly because I was furious with myself for upsetting you like that. I should have known how hurt you would be. So will you, Kate—will you trust me?' He turned away, running a hand over his face, his voice so low when he next spoke that Kate had the feeling that he was speaking to himself rather than to her. 'Heaven knows I never expected this to be so difficult.'

There was silence while Kate mulled over what he'd said. All along she'd had the feeling that there was something more behind Aaron's desire to help her, and now it seemed she could be right. She racked her brain, trying desperately to understand what it could be, then stifled a gasp as she came up with a mind-blowing explanation. Was he attracted to her? Was that the real reason why he had helped her, the reason he had kept coming into the café? Had Tony been partly right in his assessment of the situation?

Little hot and cold shivers raced up and down her spine as she faced the possibility. It would explain so much: why he seemed to watch her with that strange intensity; why he seemed to care what happened to her; why that kiss had been so devastating! Shaken by the thought, Kate could barely find the strength to speak.

'I . . . yes, Aaron. We'll leave it as it is for now, if that's what you want. I know——'

The door opened abruptly and Kate swung round, her eyes widening as she saw Jack in the doorway, or rather, saw the expression on his face. Never in all the time she had known him had she witnessed such a show of anger on his face.

Hurrying across the room, she caught hold of his arm, suddenly filled with an inexplicable fear.

'Jack! What is it? What's happened? Oh . . . it's not Chrissie, is it? Jack!'

The colour drained from her face at the thought and she swayed, clamping a hand to her mouth to stem the swift rush of fear. With a low oath Aaron hurried forwards and caught her round the shoulders, pulling her against the solid support of his body. Gratefully, Kate clung to him, needing his strength as her knees started to buckle.

For a long minute Jack stared blankly at them, then suddenly seemed to come to his senses.

'No! No, Kate. Chrissie is fine. I'm sorry, I didn't mean to alarm you like that.'

He ran a hand through his hair and Kate was worried to see that it was shaking. What had happened to cause this usually calm man so much distress? If it wasn't Chrissie then what on God's green earth was it?

'What has happened, Jack?' she asked softly, forcing herself to sound far calmer than she felt.

Jack hesitated and Kate had the strangest feeling that he was choosing his words with care before he answered, but why? What was it so hard for him to tell her?

'There has been a break-in upstairs at the flat. That's what held me up so long. I went upstairs to change when I arrived back from the hospital and discovered it.'

'Oh, no! How awful. Has much been taken?'

Jack shrugged, his face cold and grim. 'It's hard to tell. There's been quite a lot of damage done, I'm afraid. The whole place is in such a mess that it's going to take ages just to straighten it up, let alone find out what is missing.'

'Oh, Jack.'

There was a wealth of concern in Kate's soft voice and Jack smiled faintly at her before reaching out to pat her arm, his eyes strangely gentle yet filled with something she didn't quite understand, something which filled her with sudden unease. Was there something else he hadn't told her about?

'Have you called the police yet?' Aaron spoke for the first time, his voice hard as he stared at the other man.

Jack shook his head. 'No, not yet.'

'But, Jack, you must, and as soon as possible. It's the only way you'll ever catch them. I wonder when it happened. I was in—— Oh!'

In a sudden flash Kate remembered what had happened in the alley, that feeling she'd had that there had been someone there, watching her . . . or watching the entrance to the flat!

'What is it, Kate?' Aaron swung her round, studying the expression of shock on her face with narrowed, assessing eyes.

'It's just that when I was waiting round the back tonight for Jack to come home I had the funniest feeling that there was someone else there in the alley, hiding in one of the gateways. It was the main reason I came round to the casino entrance. It made me feel so uneasy.' She forced a light little laugh, but nothing could hide the shiver which raced through her body at the memory. 'If only I hadn't been such a coward

and gone to check then maybe I could have scared
the burglar off.'

'Thank heavens you didn't! Listen, Kate, I want
you to promise me that you won't ever, *ever*, do such
a crazy thing again as to stand in back alleys. There's
just no knowing what could have happened to you
tonight if he had realised you'd seen him.'

'Actually, I think he did know,' Kate said. 'When
I was running round to the front I heard stones skit-
tering along the ground. I didn't get the idea he was
too bothered about me knowing he was there. At the
time I thought he was watching me, in fact, but
obviously I was wrong. He was just waiting for me
to leave so he could get on with his rotten job.'

Jack's face went even grimmer. He shot a quick
glance at Aaron, his eyes narrowing, and Kate had
the craziest feeling that some sort of silent message
had passed between them when Aaron nodded faintly
back at him. What on earth was going on? What did
they know that she didn't?

Annoyed that they were keeping things from her,
Kate rounded on them, her green eyes brilliant with
indignation.

'OK, so what is going on? What do you two know
that I don't? Come on, tell me. I wasn't born yesterday, you know.'

'Nothing is going on, Kate. You're imagining things
because you're overwrought, that's all.'

Aaron's voice was cool, faintly amused, and
stopped Kate dead in her tracks. Was she imagining
things, allowing the fright she'd had and the drama
of it all to run away with her? She looked from one

man to another, but it was impossible to tell from either's expression if her suspicions were correct or merely fanciful. Please heaven she never came up against either of them in a game of poker, because both were a whizz at hiding their true feelings!

'Aaron is right, Kate. There's nothing going on that need worry you. There's one burglary every minute, or some sort of ridiculous figure like that, so it was on the cards, I suppose, that it could happen. Now the important thing we must decide on is what we are going to do with you.'

'Me? What do you mean? I'm going straight up to the flat this very minute to help you clear up, of course. There's no way I'm having Chrissie coming home to that sort of a mess.' Picking up her sodden coat and bag, Kate headed for the door, but Jack stepped forwards to block her way.

'No! I mean, no, I won't let you do that. You're tired, and from the look of you the only thing you need tonight is a hot bath and then bed. I'll get someone to help me tomorrow. Anyhow, you can't do anything at all until the police have been, can you?'

'I suppose not. But, Jack, what about Chrissie? I don't want her worrying about it. It's just so horrible, the thought that strangers have been searching through all your things like that.'

'She's not going to hear a word about it, Kate. Not one word. I spoke to the doctor tonight and he told me that he wants to keep her in for a few more days. Her blood-pressure is a bit high at the moment, not enough to cause concern, but he does feel that she would benefit from a few days' complete bed rest. By the time she comes home everything will be back in place and she won't need to know a thing about it.'

'Well, I suppose that's the best idea.'

'Of course it is. Now I suggest we get you settled for the night and then I can call the police and report what's happened.'

'Kate will stay at my house, of course,' Aaron said quietly.

'Oh, but I——'

'Good. That's settled, then. At least I know she'll be in safe hands.'

'You don't need to worry. I'll look after her.'

There it was again, that strange little undercurrent, that tiny inflexion in their voices. It was like playing a game, yet not having a full set of the rules and missing out on some vital piece of information. For a moment Kate tried to work out what it was that worried her about the seemingly innocent conversation, but she couldn't. Not that it mattered, of course, what sort of undercurrent was flowing when it was the words themselves which really bothered her the most. How dared they talk about her as though she were a child who needed to have decisions made for her by the grown-ups? *She* would decide where she was going to stay the night. She wouldn't just let them pack her off to Aaron's house without a by-your-leave, or even a token discussion of what she wanted to do! She refused to be handed round like an unwanted parcel.

Hands on slim hips, she glared at them both, though Aaron got the major share of the look if she was honest. 'Now look here, I can make up my own mind about where I intend to go, thank you very much. I am over twenty-one and I do have a brain in my head and a tongue in my mouth!'

Aaron raised a quizzical eyebrow, his eyes laughing at her while his face remained infuriatingly impassive. 'By my reckoning you have quite a few other attributes going for you as well as those, Kate, but point taken. If you can't stay at the flat, which I suppose is what you intended to do tonight, where would you like to go?'

The ball was well and truly back in her court, but for a blank moment Kate didn't know which way to hit it. She hadn't expected him to give in so easily to her views, and now his easy acquiescence threw her into a quandary. She bit her lips as she tried desperately to think where she should go, but it was hopeless.

'How about a hotel?' Aaron suggested, leaning back against the wall, his hands pushed casually into the pockets of his trousers so that his jacket fell open to reveal a portion of muscularly lean chest under the pale silk shirt. For a moment, the briefest heartbeat of time, Kate remembered how it had felt to be held against that chest, to rest against it and feel its solid comforting strength, before hastily pushing the memory aside. What had he just said before she got distracted...? Yes, a hotel. That was where she would go. She smiled warmly at him, grateful for the unexpected lead. It was funny, but she'd never expected him to help her out like that. She'd had the feeling he had wanted her to stay the night at his house as much as Jack so obviously did, but she'd been wrong. He was probably just as anxious to avoid the embarrassment of having her stay after this morning's little fiasco as she was.

'Yes, I think that would be the best idea, don't you?' She coloured delicately, hating what she had to say next but knowing there was no way round it. 'I've not brought much money with me, Jack, so can you lend me some just to tide me over and pay for a hotel room, please?'

'You know I would, Kate,' Jack said quietly, a trace of regret in his voice, 'but I'm afraid I've hardly any cash on me myself, and my cheque-book is buried somewhere under that mess upstairs—that is, if it hasn't been stolen. I doubt if I can find it tonight.'

'But surely you could borrow some money from the casino float, couldn't you?' Kate cried, totally nonplussed by his unexpected refusal.

''Fraid not. It's a cardinal rule that no one, not even me, borrows from the club. Perhaps Aaron can help you out.'

Aaron shook his head. 'Sorry, but no. I rushed out tonight without either my wallet or my cheque-book, I'm afraid.'

It was a conspiracy. Kate knew it, knew also that she would never in a thousand years be able to make them admit it! Snatching up her ruined coat, she slung it round her shoulders and glared at them.

'Thank you both very much, I don't think! It seems I have no option, then, but to stay at Aaron's as you suggested in the first place. How very convenient! Goodnight, Jack. I shall see you tomorrow, I expect.'

Head high, she strode out of the door, muttering a string of unladylike curses under her breath at their duplicity. Behind her she could hear Aaron speaking to Jack, his voice too low for her to make out the words, but she didn't even bother to try. Let them keep their secrets, every single one of them, and she hoped they choked them. Men! Especially one singularly infuriating specimen called Aaron Blake!

CHAPTER SEVEN

TEMPER kept Kate company as she stormed out of the casino, ignoring the curious glance the receptionist gave her with an icy hauteur. She ran down the steps and stood next to Aaron's car, tapping her foot with impatience while she waited for him to catch her up. The rain had stopped at long last, but the pavements were still wet, reflecting the light from the street lamps in sickly yellow patches. A sharp little wind was blowing, knifing through the sodden folds of cloth draped round her shoulders, and Kate shivered, pulling the damp fabric tighter round her neck. Thankfully her hair was almost dry, the silky red strands lifting in the breeze, and she raised an impatient hand to push the tickling wisps away from her face. Further down the street, a man hurried across the road, his head bowed low, his fair hair blowing wildly in the wind, but apart from that lone figure everywhere was deserted. Kate glanced round, feeling irritated that Aaron was keeping her waiting like this. Where on earth was he?

She was on the verge of marching back into the casino to see where he had got to when he appeared in the doorway and ran lightly down the steps. He smiled at her, his eyes faintly amused when he saw the mutinous curl of her soft lips, the sparks in her green eyes.

'Sorry. I didn't mean to keep you waiting. Here, hurry up and get into the car before you catch a chill. You'll be lucky to escape without one after the soaking you've had today.'

He unlocked the door and held it open while she slid inside, closing it with a mocking precision when she gave him an imperious little nod of thanks. He walked calmly round to the driver's side and climbed inside, shooting an amused glance at her while he started the engine.

'Not still angry, are you, Kate?'

'What do you think?' she snapped back waspishly, huddling deeper into the soggy folds of her ruined coat. The rain had soaked right through to the lining and she wriggled uncomfortably as it started to seep through her sweater on to her skin.

Aaron laughed, ignoring her ill temper as he set the car into gear and pulled away from the kerb. Annoyed with herself for not being able to match his composure, Kate turned her head away and stared out of the window.

The man she had noticed before crossing the street had reached the corner now and he stopped as he heard the car approaching. He waited on the kerb, his head bowed low against the wind, and Kate studied him for a moment. There was something strangely familiar about him, though for the life of her she couldn't think what it was. The street was too dimly lit and she was too far away to see his face clearly, yet she had the feeling that she knew him. Awareness tugged at her mind but couldn't seem to draw the elusive memory to the forefront.

The car turned the corner, leaving the man behind, and she shrugged the nagging little feeling aside. After all, what did it matter who he was? He wasn't the problem at the moment when she had so many other things on her mind. She was going to spend another night at Aaron's house, but was that really a wise thing to do in view of previous events? Oh, she might feel irritated right at the moment at the ease with which Jack and Aaron had outmanoeuvred her, but that wasn't a major problem. Being alone in the house with Aaron tonight might be, though!

She glanced at him, feeling the heat rush to her cheeks when she found he was watching her with an assessing look in his eyes.

'What's the matter?' she asked sharply to cover her confusion and the sudden terrifying pounding of her heart. 'Have I suddenly grown two heads or something?'

Aaron shrugged, turning his attention back to the road as they joined a string of traffic at a busy junction.

'Nothing is wrong. I was just wondering if I was going to get the silent treatment all the way home.'

'Don't you deserve it? What exactly was going on back there? What were you and Jack plotting?' Deliberately she tried to whip up her anger, knowing it was her only defence against a situation which was fast slipping out of her control.

'Why do you think there was anything going on?'

'Oh, come on! I'm not deaf, dumb and blind, so don't give me that! I *know* you were up to something, Aaron. I just don't know what it was, that's all.'

'Maybe it's better that you don't know,' he said softly, his voice so grave that for a second a shiver trailed like an icy finger down her spine.

'What do you mean?' she asked, her mouth suddenly dry as dust so that her voice sounded hoarsely unfamiliar even to her own ears.

'Nothing. I was just talking for talking's sake, that's all. Anything is better than a cold silence. Look, Kate, I know you are still upset about this morning but I thought we had managed to iron most of it out before in the casino.'

It was obvious what he was alluding to and Kate felt her pulse leap and her heart start to hammer hard against her chest as the memory of just how they had 'ironed' things out came rushing back. She looked down, twisting her fingers together in her lap while she tried to find some non-committal answer to defuse the sudden tension. She was going back to Aaron's house to stay the night and she didn't want to be reminded of how she had felt before in his arms. It would be too easy to let the attraction she felt for him run away with her.

'Kate, stop it.' He reached out and squeezed her fingers, his touch firm and gentle. 'There's nothing to worry about. I'm not taking you back to the house to seduce you.'

How could he read her so well, look inside her mind and see her thoughts with such clarity? Kate didn't know, but she wished desperately that he couldn't do it. She looked up, forcing a smooth little smile to her lips to hide the anxiety gnawing insistently away at her.

'I didn't think you were. I'm sorry, I suppose I'm still rather embarrassed about what I did this morning. It was silly of me to run away like that. When all's said and done it got me absolutely nowhere, did it? I could have saved myself a soaking if I'd acted a bit more sensibly.' There was a touch of wry self-mockery in her voice and Aaron laughed, the deep, rich sound filling the car.

'You most definitely could, and saved me from getting one too for that matter.'

'What on earth do you mean?' Startled, Kate turned slightly in her seat to look at him.

'Just that I managed to get half drowned standing outside the hospital watching for you. I knew very well that if you spotted the car there was a good chance you would take off again, so I parked it a few streets away and spent the best part of the day skulking behind a gate post. I got a few strange looks, I can tell you. Was I glad when Jack finally showed up and promised to phone me if he heard from you!'

He laughed again, ruefully making light of what he had done, but Kate knew she would never forgive herself for causing him so much trouble.

'I'm sorry,' she said softly, her voice filled with remorse. 'I just didn't think. I was so angry, so upset, that I never thought any further than getting out of the car and away from you. I . . . I never dreamt that you would do that, stand out in all that rain, watching for me. Can you ever forgive me for being such a nuisance?'

'There's nothing to forgive, Kate. Nothing you should feel guilty about. Oh, I admit I was furious this morning when you took off, but it was as much with myself for being so crass and insensitive as with you. Now I realise it was probably for the best, as it helped clear the air and gave us both time to think.' He shot her a quick smile as he stopped the car at the junction, and Kate felt her heart melt at the tender expression on his face. How could he do that, at one minute make her rip-roaringly angry then at the next make her feel like a marshmallow? She shook her head slightly to clear the hazy fog which seemed to cloud her brain. She couldn't afford to have her thoughts clouded and her ideas hazy when she was around Aaron Blake. That would really be asking for trouble!

'Let's make a pact, shall we, Kate, that tonight we forget about all the bickering, all the uncertainty, and try to make the best of the hours that are left? I know a nice little restaurant quite near here, so how about you and I going there for a meal and a couple of hours' relaxation?'

He turned the car expertly into the flow of traffic and Kate sat silently while he drove along the street, mulling over the suggestion. In other circumstances she would have agreed gladly to the offer, but surely there was one very important detail he had overlooked.

Biting back a small chuckle of laughter, she said mildly, 'Well, I don't think that would be a good idea, Aaron, in the circumstances.'

He shot her a quick glance, his eyes narrowed. 'What circumstances? You're not still worrying about what I said this morning, surely? Look, Kate, I've already told you I didn't mean a single word of it!'

'I know, I know. There's really no need to get all het up about it. That wasn't what I meant at all.'

She glanced down, anxious to hide the amusement she felt from him for a few minutes longer. After all, surely he deserved to be paid back just the smallest bit for the way he had manipulated her back at the casino.

'Then what is it?'

With a jerky movement, he eased the car out of the traffic and pulled in to the kerb. He turned to face her, annoyance showing briefly on his face before his expression softened.

'You're not worrying about your clothes, are you, Kate? I know your coat is soaked but, believe me, sweetheart, you still look far more beautiful than any of the other women who will be there.'

'Thank you, but how I look isn't the problem. Lack of money is!' She grinned at him, her eyes sparkling with laughter. 'I seem to remember you stating ever so clearly just a few minutes ago that you'd come out without a bean in your pocket tonight. So, how do you propose to pay for this meal you've offered me? I don't fancy washing dishes if you can't pay the bill, do you?'

There was a brief, expectant silence, then Aaron laughed, the sound rippling warmly round the car. Reaching out, he pulled her to him and brushed a quick kiss against her brow. He tilted her chin up as he smiled down at her and Kate felt her blood quicken.

'Do you know what you are, Kate Warren?'

'No,' she whispered, all too conscious of his closeness and the effect it was having on her bloodstream. 'What am I?'

'A scheming, conniving little minx, that's what!'

'Oh . . . Oh . . . well, just as long as you remember it, Aaron, then there won't be a problem.' She pulled away, running a hand briskly over her ruffled hair, not quite able to make up her mind whether to be vexed or pleased by the description! 'I don't know if you deserve it after what you just said, but I *did* have a suggestion to make.'

'What was it?' Sitting back in his seat, Aaron crossed his arms and looked at her with mock sternness.

'That you let me buy you some fish and chips.' She reached over to pluck the note and scattered silver from the dashboard where she'd flung it that morning. 'This should just about cover it at London prices, might even run to a cheap bottle of wine if we're lucky. So is it a deal?'

'You're on. Best deal I've had all day. Fish and chips it is, Kate, coming right up.'

He restarted the car and drove down the street and Kate sat back in her seat, feeling happier than she'd felt in months. At the back of her mind a tiny thought was nibbling, gnawing insistently away at the edges of the quiet feeling of pleasure, but with a steely determination Kate shut it away. She didn't want to think about it now, didn't want to think about the fact that she was getting far too involved with this man than she ought to. She wanted to enjoy the next few hours in Aaron's company. She would worry about the wisdom of it all later.

*   *   *

Kate licked the last trace of salt off her fingers then crumpled up the greasy paper, smiling as she lifted it off the delicate china plate. Fish and chips, still wrapped in paper, but served on best Sèvres porcelain—well, that was a first for her even if it was commonplace for the man sitting opposite her!

She glanced up at him, her eyes lingering on the dark hair which fell so carelessly across his brow. Under the bright kitchen light she could see glints of silver in the dark strands at his temples, could see the tiny lines fanned from the corners of his eyes. How old was he? Thirty-five, approaching forty? It was hard to tell, hard to put a precise age on him when she knew so little about him. This was the second night she would spend under Aaron's roof, accepting his hospitality, yet what exactly did she know about him? Oh, she knew he was a successful businessman, that he was tough and a formidable opponent, but what did she know about him personally? What did she know about the real man behind the polished exterior?

Gathering up the crumpled papers, Kate walked over to the bin and shoved them inside before rinsing the plates in the sudsy water, her actions purely reflex because her mind was still centred on the man sitting quietly at the table. He was holding a glass of wine in his hand, idly swirling the pale liquid round and round the fine crystal, obviously lost in his own thoughts, and suddenly Kate knew she had to know more about this man who had come so unexpectedly into her life.

He looked up suddenly to catch her watching him, and Kate turned hurriedly away and busied herself drying the plates before stacking them in the cupboard. She hung the towel back on its rack, taking her time smoothing the creases out of the soft terry cloth to give herself time to think. If she wanted to know more about Aaron, then she would have to ask him, yet suddenly, strangely she was afraid to begin, afraid of where her curiosity could lead to.

'Well, Kate, that was a good idea of yours. I doubt if I could have enjoyed any restaurant meal more than I did that.' His voice was low, easy, and Kate chided herself for allowing her own irrational fears to run away with her. After all, surely it was only natural that she should be curious about him and his background? She smiled at him, turning away to fill the kettle before returning to the table.

'Good. I'm glad you enjoyed it. Far better than having to wash up at that restaurant as we so nearly had to do, I reckon.'

He chuckled deeply, tilting the glass to swallow the last of the wine, and Kate found her eyes locked to the strong, bronzed column of his throat, found that for some reason she couldn't seem to look away. Fire licked through her veins and she clenched her hands together in her lap as she held back the almost overwhelming urge to run her fingers down the long line of his throat and caress that firm golden skin.

Aaron set the glass back on the table, a hint of puzzlement in his gaze as he noticed the tension on her face, the rigidity of her slender body. Desperately Kate tried to make herself relax, not wanting him to know just what an effect he could have on her by the simple action of drinking! Heaven help her, but she must be more tired and strung out than she'd imagined.

The kettle came to the boil, hissing steam across the quiet room, and Kate shot to her feet in relief. A cup of nice hot tea was just what she needed to get her wayward emotions on even keel again. Maybe that single glass of wine she'd just drunk had been more potent than she'd realised. It was a good job that she'd had only the one or heaven alone knew where a second or third might have led to!

She lifted a cup down from the cupboard then paused to shoot a question over her shoulder.

'Do you want a drink . . . tea or coffee?'

'No, thanks. I'll stick to the wine, I think.'

He poured another glass of the pale liquid then raised it, his eyes locked to hers. 'Here's to us, Kate . . . and whatever the future may bring.'

He sipped the wine as his gaze travelled slowly over her face and Kate had to look away, feeling suddenly breathless. She made the tea then carried it across to the table, her hand trembling so that tea spilled into the saucer and pooled round the bottom of the cup. What had been in his eyes just then, what emotion? Kate couldn't identify it, yet something inside her reacted to it. When Aaron looked at her that way, his eyes so deep, so dark, so full of secrets, it made her feel things she didn't want to feel, not tonight when they were alone together in this house. Tonight she wanted to be calm and rational, to accept his hospitality and nothing else—nothing like the promises she'd seen burning briefly, tantalisingly in his eyes.

She raised the cup to her lips and sipped the tea, feeling it inching its way down her tight throat in a hot stream, but nothing could equal the heat racing through her veins.

'Relax, Kate. You're all tensed up.'

Aaron caught hold of her free hand, his long fingers stroking over the smooth skin before moving round to settle against the throbbing, jerky little pulse in her wrist. 'What's the matter, sweetheart? You're not frightened of me, are you?'

When he put it like that Kate knew her answer had to be a great resounding 'no', but something made her hesitate about giving it. It wasn't fear of *him* that she was feeling, but fear of what emotions he could unleash inside her. Yet how else could she explain her tension, the pounding surge of blood beating through her veins? Aaron Blake was an extremely attractive and experienced man who must have had more than his fair share of women, so how long would it take for him to add two to two and come up with a four-thousand-dollar answer? She didn't want him to do that, to realise just how greatly he affected her. It made her far too vulnerable to him.

She took a slow, deep breath then spat the lie out quickly before the bitter taste of it could choke her.

'Yes, just a bit. Surely it's only natural for me to feel a bit on edge? You've been very kind to me, Aaron, but I really don't know anything about you, do I? Last night I was still in shock over Chrissie's accident, but now that I can think more clearly I'm wondering if I am doing the right thing staying here.

Why, for all I know you could be Bluebeard's grandson, couldn't you?'

Aaron laughed at the wry mockery in her voice, and Kate breathed a little easier as she realised she had successfully managed to distract him.

'Mmm, I suppose I could be, and here you are, all alone with me. What a thought, Kate! Still, rest easy. I can assure you that I don't have a lurid past, nor any leanings towards a lurid future either. I suppose I could supply you with a list of referees who would testify as to my impeccable honesty and the fact that I never attack defenceless women, but do I really need to go that far? What do you want to know about me, Kate? Ask away if it will make you feel any easier.'

He raised the glass to his lips, his blue eyes sparkling with amusement, and Kate smiled at him in relief. This was going to be far simpler than she'd hoped it would.

'Oh, just the usual things, I suppose. How old you are, if you have any family, how you came to be in business in such a big way. Anything you care to tell me.'

'Well, you asked for it, Kate, so don't blame me if you get bored! To start at the beginning, I'm thirty-five and I was born and brought up in London in an area not too different from where you were working. My father worked on the docks until ill health forced him to retire. After that, life was a struggle, and I'd be a liar if I tried to make out that I was an angel in my youth, but I never got into any serious trouble. Oh, I had a few close shaves but somehow always managed to wriggle myself out of them. After my

father died my mother supported us by cleaning at
one of the office blocks in the City, and it was through
her that I got my first break. She heard that they
needed an office junior and sent me round to apply
for the job even before it was advertised. I must admit
that I was reluctant to go. Boys from my sort of background didn't go for jobs like that but, well, she
wanted me to try for it so I went and, amazingly
enough, got it. It was the turning-point for me. Suddenly I found myself in a whole new world, and that
was it. I was hooked on the excitement and the power
of it, the thrill of seeing millions of pounds change
hands within the space of hours. I listened hard and
I learned, everything from the ground up, and used
any tips I gleaned to make investments for myself.
Obviously they were small ones at first, but I soon
found that I had a flair for making money, an instinct
for which deals were sound and which weren't. I saved
every penny I made, then took a gamble and set up
on my own. Now Blake International is one of the
ten top investment corporations in the world.'

There was the ring of pride in his deep voice which
Kate could appreciate. He must have worked hard to
get where he was today. He might have a flair for
making money, but there was no way he could have
done it without total commitment.

'So where do you go next? Will you make that
investment in Liverpool or what?'

He shrugged. 'Probably. I've yet to iron out all the
details, but yes, I think it could be a sound investment
both for myself and the city. I like Liverpool, Kate.
I like the people, the warmth, the humour. Oh, it has

its faults like any big city, but there's a certain determination there, a desire not to let the odds beat you which I admire. But how about you, Kate? Will you go back once this is all over?'

'I don't know.' She glanced down at the cup, tilting the cooling dregs of tea from side to side in a tiny tidal wave. 'I don't know if it will be worth my while going back there when I have no job to go back to.'

'You think Manetti will carry out his threat and hire someone else, then?' Aaron's voice was grim and Kate shivered slightly as she heard it, heard the underlying edge of steel. Aaron Blake hadn't got where he was by being soft. He would be a bad man to cross. She set the cup down with a sharp little clatter, wondering why the thought of him being a ruthless adversary was so disturbing. It made the kindness he had shown to her seem even stranger than ever. Why had he helped her? Had it really been because he was attracted to her? Suddenly Kate was far less certain that was the answer.

'Kate?'

He prompted her to answer and Kate shoved the questions to the back of her mind to deal with later.

'Probably. Let's just say that things have been strained between us for a few weeks now. Tony seemed to think that I should be a bit more grateful to him for giving me the job and that I should show him . . . well, show him special favours.'

Colour filled her cheeks at the admission and Aaron swore softly, slamming the glass down on the table with such force that Kate was surprised the fragile stem didn't snap.

'Hell, Kate, how did you stand it? It was bad enough those few days I was in the café listening to him, but how did you put up with it day in and day out?'

Kate shrugged, her eyes guarded, her voice tinged with bitterness.

'Beggars can't be choosers. It's a true saying and I was glad of the job, Aaron. I know it wasn't much, but when that's all there is then you hang on to it and put up with the drawbacks. Mind you, it wasn't all bad. I soon learned how to handle Tony and I enjoyed meeting the people. Most of them were very kind to me. It was unfortunate that you came in on such a bad week!'

'If you don't go back—and I hope you don't, Kate, at least not to that café—what will you do? Will you let Jack find you a job here?' He smiled briefly at the surprise in her wide green eyes. 'Oh, yes, he told me that he'd offered to do so on more than one occasion but that you were too stubborn to let him help you out. You wanted to be independent, or so he said.'

What else had Jack told him? Ice slithered down Kate's spine at the thought of what Jack might have told Aaron about her. She stood up, walking jerkily to the sink to wash the cup, knowing that the very last thing she wanted was for Aaron to find out about her past.

'Jack shouldn't have been talking about me,' she said coldly. 'He had no right to be telling you things about me.'

'Jack said nothing apart from that, Kate, and I already know to my cost just how stubborn you can be.'

Was he telling the truth? Kate swung round, searching his face for...what? Scorn, contempt, distaste, all the emotions she'd seen before on other people's faces when they had found out who she was and what she'd done. The seconds raced past but Kate could find no trace of any of those ugly emotions on Aaron's face or in the depths of his eyes. She should have known that Jack would never betray her secrets like that.

'I'm sorry,' she said at last, her voice breaking the strained silence which filled the room. 'I guess I'm more tired than I thought I was. I'm starting to make mountains out of even the tiniest molehills. If you don't mind, Aaron, I think I'll go up to bed now. Shall I use the same room as last night?'

'Yes, of course. I've left some things on the bed for you. Just help yourself to whatever you need.'

'Thank you. Aren't you coming up yet?' She glanced at her watch, then back to him. 'It's getting late.'

'Is that an offer, Kate?'

He stood up and came towards her, stopping just a few feet away, and Kate felt herself go rigid as he stared quietly down into her face. 'Well, Kate, is it?'

His breath whispered over her skin, warming her flesh, stirring the soft tendrils of hair at her temples, and Kate closed her eyes as she fought against the hot yearning flooding through her body. Had it been an invitation, an unconscious plea to him? She didn't

know, didn't even know how to answer. At that
moment she wanted nothing more than to agree and
have this one glorious night in his arms—one night
to set against a thousand other lonely ones. Would
that really be so wrong?

'Kate?'

There was seduction in the velvet tones, magic in
the tingling feel of his hands tracing lightly up and
down her arms, and Kate prayed desperately for
guidance to make the right decision.

'It will be good between us, Kate. You'll see.'

Kate gasped and her eyes flew open while her mind
ricocheted back in time one whole long year. For a
crazy moment her vision blurred and she could no
longer see Aaron standing in front of her. All she
could see was Jonathan, his pale eyes glittering with
excitement, his voice husky as he said those very same
words to her. How many times had he said them,
cajoling, persuading, convincing her to agree to his
pleas? Kate didn't know, didn't even care as cold
reality flooded through her body and washed away
the heat of passion.

She blinked rapidly, clearing the ghostly vision from
her mind, seeing once more the man standing in front
of her.

'No,' she said clearly. 'I'm sorry, Aaron, but no.'

It was the right decision, the right answer, but as
Kate walked slowly from the room she wished she
hadn't had to give it.

CHAPTER EIGHT

DAWN was breaking, trailing pale grey fingers against a darker grey sky, but Kate was already awake. She stood by the window, huddled into the soft terry-cloth robe Aaron had lent her, her cheek resting against the misty coldness of the glass as she looked out.

Beyond the shadowy garden the first stirrings of a new day were showing, the first signs that people were waking up to see what it would bring. What would it bring for her? Another day of uncertainty, of fear that today would be the day that Aaron found out about her past? Suddenly Kate knew she couldn't face another day like that.

All night long she'd been tossing and turning, sleeping fitfully, her mind too full of ghosts and echoes to let her rest. For months now she had held back the memories, forced them from her mind, yet last night it was as though a door had opened and everything had come rushing back.

As she had lain there in that no man's land somewhere between sleep and wakefulness, Kate had gone over everything that had happened and finally come to terms with it. For a year she had given lip-service to the fact that Jonathan had been the guilty one, yet deep down she had always held herself to blame in some way. She had seen the contempt on other people's faces and judged herself accordingly. Now, however, Kate had finally realised the truth: that she was the innocent victim. Jonathan had been the guilty one. The only thing she had been guilty of was of loving him, and now even that was a thing of the past. If she was to go on and make a life for herself then she had to put it all behind her: had to tell Aaron everything, every single sordid detail. If he was shocked and rejected her, then surely it would be better if it happened now rather than later, before these tender new emotions budding inside her had blossomed into love?

With a sigh, Kate turned away from the window, stumbling slightly as her foot caught in the loose folds of the robe which reached past her ankles. Her flailing arm caught against a heavy marble statue standing on a nearby table and it fell to the floor with a thud. Cursing herself for her clumsiness, Kate stooped to pick it up, her fingers tracing over the cold, hard stone to check for any damage, but fortunately it was quite unscathed. She set it back on the table, turning it round till it stood at exactly the same angle as before, then glanced round in surprise as the door was flung abruptly open.

'Are you all right?'

Aaron stood in the doorway, his dark hair mussed, his blue eyes hazy, the shadow of stubble darkening his jaw. He was still wearing the clothes he had worn the night before, but now the silk shirt and perfectly tailored trousers were as rumpled as if he had slept in them. For a moment Kate stared at him in silence, wondering what he'd been doing since she'd left him to go to bed. She had never seen him looking so

dishevelled before, or so disturbingly attractive! With
the shirt part opened across his tanned chest and his
dark hair falling rakishly over his brow he was a sight
to make any red-blooded female's heart beat a little
faster, and Kate's was definitely no exception. Her
red corpuscles were just as active as anyone's!

'Kate? Are you all right? I heard a noise. Have you
hurt yourself?' Concern tinged his deep voice as he
advanced across the room, and Kate hastily shook
herself out of her trance. She forced a smile to her
lips, desperately trying to stem the sudden hot rush
of blood which was surging through her veins, but
nothing seemed to be able to cool the heat.

'I ... I'm fine. I just knocked the statue over, that's
all. You don't need to worry though, it's not
damaged.'

'To hell with the statue! Are you all right? It didn't
fall on you, did it?'

His eyes traced swiftly down the length of her
slender body in the loosely belted robe, and Kate felt
the colour rise quickly to her cheeks. How could he
do that? Make her so aware of him just by a look or
a simple gesture? It had never happened before with
any man, not even Jonathan, and it always made her
feel so confused and sort of tingly up her backbone!
What on earth was the matter with her? She acted like
a gauche teenager every time Aaron Blake came near
her, not a mature and sensible woman of twenty-two!

She drew in a deep breath, fighting to keep the confusion out of her voice as she spoke. 'No, I'm fine,
really. But what about you? You look as though

you've been out on the tiles all night! What have you been up to?'

Aaron shrugged, leaning against the wall while he looked out of the window, his face in profile looking faintly grim as though something was troubling him.

'I couldn't sleep, that's all. I spent most of the night in the study with a bottle of whisky for company. That probably explains my less than clean-cut, debonair appearance this morning.'

'Well, that was silly. Whisky doesn't solve anything.'

'Probably not, but it certainly helps dull the senses . . . and the pain.'

There was little doubting what he meant and Kate looked down, twisting the belt of the robe nervously between her trembling fingers. What could she say? How could she explain why she had made such a decision last night without telling him everything? Suddenly Kate knew she wasn't ready to tell him everything . . . just yet.

'Stop it, Kate. Stop taking all the blame on yourself. You made a decision last night and I respect you for it. If I had a sleepless night then that's my problem, not yours. Now, how about telling me why you are up at this unearthly hour of . . .' he peered at his watch, narrowing his eyes to bring the digits into focus '. . . five-thirty! Good lord. Surely you're not usually such an early riser, are you?'

There was a teasing lightness in his voice and Kate responded gratefully to it, realising that he was trying to put her at ease again.

'Of course I am. In fact I come from a long line of early risers, I'll have you know! I'm at my best in the morning.'

'Are you, indeed? Well, that *is* something I must remember for future reference.'

His tone put a whole new emphasis on her words and Kate felt her face turn crimson. She spun round, hurrying towards the door, feeling suddenly breathless at the shocking images which flooded into her mind. Behind her Aaron laughed, softly, deeply, the sound filling the room with intimacy.

'One day you'll have to stop running, Kate.'

Kate stopped, her hand gripping hold of the doorknob as she shot a quick look over her shoulder.

'I don't know what you mean. Stop running where?'

'Away from me, sweetheart. One day I'm going to catch you, so why not face the fact?'

'What, and save you the trouble? No chance! The only way you're ever going to catch me, Aaron Blake, unless I choose to let you, is with a great big net! Now, I think I'll go and make us both some coffee. I think we could do with a cup, and you rather more than me from the sound of it. That whisky seems to have had more effect on you than you realise!'

With a toss of her red hair, Kate walked out of the door and hurried along the landing. Behind her came the soft tread of footsteps half muffled by the thick pile of the carpet, but she didn't stop.

'I let you go last night, Kate, but next time I might not be so willing to do so.'

Kate reached the bottom of the stairs and stopped, tilting her head to look up at the man standing at the top.

'Next time, Aaron, I might not ask you to.'

Her voice was soft, the words gentle, yet carrying all the impact of a bullet as they hit home. Kate stood for a moment watching the shock which crossed his face, then calmly turned and headed for the kitchen. If Aaron Blake thought he was going to have things all his own way then he was in for a shock!

The coffee was ready, filling the kitchen with a tantalising aroma. Sniffing appreciatively, Kate picked up the pot and filled two beakers with the fragrant liquid, smiling to herself as she quite deliberately left Aaron's black. He usually drank it white, thick with cream and heavy with sugar, but this morning he was getting it hot and strong and black whether he liked it or not! After all, he surely needed something to combat all that whisky and the aftermaths of shock!

Placing the mugs carefully on to a matching tray, Kate carried them upstairs, pausing outside the door to Aaron's bedroom. She had half expected him to follow her down to the kitchen, but there'd been no sign of him while she was making the coffee. Perhaps he had decided to get changed into fresh clothes before he came down. She tapped briskly on his door, murmuring in annoyance when he didn't answer. She wanted him to drink the coffee now while it was still hot, so there was no way she was going to leave it outside the door. She would have to go in and see that he knew it was ready.

Easing the door open, she stepped inside the room, her eyes widening as she caught sight of the figure sprawled across the bed. Far from getting changed as she'd imagined, he was still wearing the same rumpled shirt and trousers, and obviously fast asleep. Was he going to regret it later when he awoke with a heavy head and a throat like sandpaper! She couldn't leave him to such a fate, now, could she? She would have to wake him up and make him drink the coffee.

With a determined gleam in her eyes Kate walked over to the bed and set the tray down on the bedside table with a noisy little clatter. Aaron groaned, mumbling irritably under his breath as if the sudden noise had annoyed him, but surely a bit of irritation was a small price to pay to stave off a massive hangover. It was regrettable, but sometimes one did have to be cruel to be kind. Kate bent down and placed her hand on his shoulder to shake him firmly.

'Come on, Aaron,' she ordered in her most rousing tone. 'Drink this while it's still hot. It will do you good.'

He stirred again, moving restlessly on the crumpled covers, but his eyes stayed firmly closed, the thick, dark lashes fanned against the lightly tanned skin of his cheeks. He looked so different lying there with his eyes closed and his face unguarded, so strangely vulnerable, that suddenly Kate found all her determination to wake him up and feed him coffee wavering. Perhaps it would be better to let him sleep off the effects of the previous night rather than disturb him, after all.

Her hand softened against his shoulder, her fingers resting against the hard, warm muscles, unconsciously caressing the firm flesh rather than shaking it, and his lips curved into a tiny smile of pleasure. For a long moment Kate stared down at him, studying the way his hair grew in a slight peak off his broad brow, the way his ears lay in a neat curve against his well-shaped head. She knew she should leave the room and let him sleep, not stand here staring at him, yet something held her spellbound. Surely there was no harm in stealing these few precious minutes to look her fill at a man who had become so very important to her.

Slowly her eyes slid down the length of his body, tracing the clean lines, the hard muscles, the lean strength of his long limbs, before sliding back up for one last look at his face, and she gasped aloud in shocked dismay.

His eyes were open, their blue depths glittering as he watched her and saw the play of emotions which crossed her face.

'Hello, Kate.'

For one timeless moment Kate met his gaze, drowning in the sapphire depths which seemed to be filled with secrets, before forcing herself to look away. She looked round the room, searching for something to explain her presence, though she doubted if anything could have truly explained her reasons for standing there watching him when she scarcely understood them herself. Her eyes focused on the cooling coffee standing untouched on the tray, and she snatched up the mug she'd poured for him and held it out towards him.

'Coffee . . . I brought you some coffee. Here, drink it up while it's still hot.'

Aaron took the mug from her trembling fingers, smiling faintly as he set it back down again on the tray. Reaching out, he caught hold of her hand and slid his fingers slowly up the slender length of her arm under the loose sleeve of the robe.

'I don't want coffee, Kate. I hate to disillusion you, but coffee isn't the remedy for what ails me at present.'

'It isn't?'

Her voice was strained, husky, so low that she wondered if he had heard her tentative question, then knew he had when he grinned wickedly up at her. It was like the four-minute warning, the alarm sounding before a nuclear explosion, and Kate knew she should take heed and run for cover, but she didn't! All her good intentions, all the sensible warnings that every mother instilled in her daughter, fled abruptly from her head as his fingers continued their light stroking of her flesh. Flash-fire raced along her veins, burning hotly, making her whole body ache as his fingers spread to cup the delicate bones of her elbow and rub them softly.

'No, Kate. I don't want coffee, or any other kind of remedy. Just you, you're the only thing I need.'

'Aaron!'

His name gasped from her lips, a tiny explosion of startled sound and aching feeling which echoed through the sudden silence and shocked her rigid. She stared down at him, her eyes a brilliant vivid green as she saw the tenderness in his expression, the unmistakable longing.

'Just you, Kate,' he repeated softly, his fingers sliding smoothly down her arm to close around her hand and pull her towards him. 'Kill or cure, you are the only remedy I need.'

She fell against him, her softness meeting the hard strength of his body in a sudden shocking contact which sent the flames flaring higher and higher along her veins. Kate gasped, pushing against his chest so that she could keep a tiny space between them while she tried to think and get her reeling senses into some sort of order.

'No, Aaron, no! You can't do this. You're tired, letting the whisky think for you. It's wrong!'

'Shhh.'

He pressed a finger against her lips, stroking it back and forth across the soft, moist flesh, and Kate fell silent while every single cell in her body screamed out wildly.

'How can it be wrong, Kate? Does it feel wrong? Does this?'

His lips trailed along her cheekbone, then down the soft smooth skin to nibble delicately at the hollow in her neck, and Kate gasped in pleasure. Slowly, deliberately he slid his mouth up the slopes again and kissed her eyelids, gently teasing the corners with tiny butterfly-soft kisses. 'Or this, Kate?' The question whispered from him just an instant before his mouth swooped down to brush a tormenting shower of kisses against her lips, and Kate moaned softly, helplessly.

'Is it wrong, Kate? Shall I stop and let you go again?'

His mouth hovered over hers, his lips brushing gently against hers as he spoke, and Kate shuddered at the exquisite sensation the light contact created. Deep down she knew she should accept his offer to let her go now while she was still able, yet something stopped her.

For a long moment she stared up into his face, seeing the unmistakable longing, the fires barely banked in his eyes. She hadn't wanted this to happen, not yet, not until she had had a chance to talk to him and tell him everything, but suddenly Kate knew that she wanted nothing more than to stay here in his arms and let him love her.

'No, Aaron. No, I don't want you to let me go.'

The words echoed from her mouth into his and she felt him shudder. With a dizzying speed he rolled her over on the bed, his eyes deep and dark and strangely shadowed as they met hers.

'Kate...sweet, sweet, Kate.'

Her name whispered from him like a litany, a prayer, and Kate reacted blindly to it. Arching upwards, she pressed herself against him, feeling the way his muscles contracted in a violent spasm as her hand slid down the broad slopes of his shoulders to the buttons on his shirt. Slowly, delicately, she worked them free and pressed hungry little kisses to the bare, warm hardness of his chest until Aaron could stand the torment no longer. With a low groan he lifted her head and took her mouth in a kiss of such intensity that she was lost.

Passion flared between them, burned them up and consumed them until they were both its masters and its disciples. It was agony and ecstasy, joy and sadness, every single emotion focused into one marvellous moment. Nothing mattered any more, not the past, not the future, nothing but the joy of being in Aaron's arms. In that instant Kate knew that she never wanted him to let her go... ever again.

The light woke her. Kate rolled over, raising her hand to shield her eyes from the glare of light spilling in through the window. For a long moment she stared round the room, her eyes lingering on the unfamiliar furnishings before drifting back to the rumpled bed. Colour flared in her cheeks and her breathing quickened as the memories came flooding back, memories of the hours she and Aaron had lain together making love with an intensity which had bordered on desperation.

Breathless, trembling, she closed her eyes, feeling again the touch of his hands against her skin, the taste of his mouth on her lips, the scent which was so intrinsically his.

'Kate? Are you all right?'

The soft-voiced question caught her by surprise and her eyes flew open as she turned her head. Aaron was standing in the doorway, his expression one of concern as he studied her taut features, the heightened colour in her cheeks. Kate pulled herself up against the pillows, searching frantically for something to say, something to ease the sudden tension which filled the room and arced between them, but frankly could come up with nothing equal to the occasion. What did you say to a man who had held you in his arms and made passionate love to you, a man who knew every curve and line of your body, a man who was still a virtual stranger? Kate's experience of life hadn't prepared her for this sort of situation, the morning after a night of passion, and now words failed her. All she could do was stare at him, everything she felt, every uncertainty, showing on her face.

'Stop it, Kate! Stop it right now!'

With a low, muttered oath Aaron strode across the room and sat down on the side of the bed to take her hands and hold them firmly.

'You have nothing to feel guilty or ashamed about, Kate. What we did before was beautiful, not sordid!'

There was anger in his deep voice and in the way his long fingers tightened painfully round hers, and Kate knew she couldn't let him misinterpret the confusion she felt for regret. She smiled at him, her face gentle, her eyes tender as she stared into his face.

'I don't feel either guilty or ashamed, Aaron,' she said softly. 'I'm just not used to this sort of situation, that's all. I really don't know what I should say or how I should handle it. None of the books on etiquette cover this sort of thing, I'm afraid, and as I've never done this before, slept with a man I've known for only a few days, I don't know what the rules are. I mean, should I shake your hand and thank you sweetly then quietly leave, or what?'

Aaron laughed, his eyes dancing in amusement at the absurdity of the question. 'Definitely not! There's no way I'm letting you leave just yet. But seriously,

Kate, does the length of time we've known each other really matter that much? Would it have made any difference to what we felt before if we'd met last year rather than last week? Some things are meant to be, Kate, and our lovemaking was one of them.'

He bent forwards to brush a light kiss over her lips and Kate felt the last of the tension ease from her body. He was right, of course. Those hours in his arms had been perfect, and nothing as mundane as a measurement of time could alter that.

'Mmm, I suppose you're right.'

'I know I'm right. Now come along, up you get, unless you would like me to join you there again.'

There was a wicked gleam in the look Aaron levelled at her and Kate felt her blood quicken. She slid slowly down on the pillows, stretching her body under the light covering sheet, loving the way his eyes followed the movement and lingered.

'Well, I don't know. I mean, do you think it would be a good idea? You might be tired, and I don't know if it would be advisable to overtax your strength like that.'

'Overtax my... I'll give you overtaxing my strength, you saucy minx! By the time I've finished with you, lady, you'll be begging for mercy!'

He took a step towards the bed, then groaned sharply as the telephone suddenly rang shrilly in the hall below.

'Saved by the bell. Your punishment will have to wait till later.'

'Promises, promises,' Kate answered saucily as he reluctantly left the room. For a moment she lay quite still, listening to the muted sound of his voice echoing up from the hall, then with a tiny sigh pushed the covers back and climbed out of the bed. Though she hated to admit it, maybe it had been a good thing that the phone had rung just then. From the look of the sun high in the sky it was already quite late in the day, and she wanted to go over to the flat to help Jack clear up before she visited the hospital. Tempting as the thought of waiting in the bed for Aaron to come back was, duty called. She would have to forgo till later the pleasure of seeing what form his 'punishment' would take!

Picking up the robe from where it had fallen to the floor, Kate slid her arms into the sleeves and knotted the belt round her waist. She walked to the dressing-table and picked up a brush, pausing with it halfway to her hair while she studied her face. She looked the same as she always did, the small, neat features unchanged, yet there was a glow to her face, a hectic glitter in her green eyes which she'd never seen before. For the first time in a year she looked happy, and it was all thanks to one man ... Aaron Blake.

He had come into her life out of the blue and taken it over with an ease which was almost frightening, yet what did either of them truly know about the other? Surely now was the time for them to talk, now before they drifted into an even greater intimacy? Now was the time when she must tell him everything about her past.

She set the brush down, her hand shaking so that it clattered against the glass-covered surface of the dressing-table. Cold dread was stealing through her

limbs and she pulled the robe tighter round her body.
At that moment Kate would have given anything not
to have to face Aaron and tell him about the trial,
but she had to. If she wanted to build a future then
it had to be on the solid rock of honesty and not on
the quicksand of deception.

She left the bedroom, her feet slowing as she
reached the hall. There was no sign of Aaron by the
telephone and she hesitated, wondering where to find
him. A faint noise came from along the hall and Kate
walked towards it, halting uncertainly in the doorway
to what was evidently his study.

Standing at the desk, Aaron was briskly packing
papers into a slim briefcase, his fingers whisking
through the stacked folders with a deftness which
seemed strangely at variance with the troubled
expression on his face. What was wrong with him?
What had happened to cause that look of anguish on
his face?

Kate hurried into the room and across to the desk,
catching hold of his hand to stop the hasty, silent
packing.

'What's happened? Is there something wrong,
Aaron?'

For a long minute he looked at her, his eyes dark
and filled with . . . what? Regret, sorrow? Kate didn't
know, but whatever it was it made the ice flow a little
colder through her veins. She dropped his hand and
stepped back a pace, suddenly uncertain that she
wanted to hear his answer. She felt afraid, but of
what? Of the expression on his face and in his eyes?
That didn't make any kind of sense.

'Something has come up, Kate, and I have to go out unexpectedly. I'm sorry.'

There it was again, in his voice this time, that hint of tension, that thread of some emotion which made her stomach lurch and her heart beat a little faster. Kate pushed her hands deep into the pockets of the robe to hide their sudden tremble and walked to the window, making a great show of peering out into the garden while she tried to make sense of the whole situation. Aaron had been fine before, so what had that phone call been about to cause this sort of reaction in him?

From behind her came the sound of the case locks being snapped shut and Kate stiffened as she sensed rather than heard him coming up behind her. She shot a glance over her shoulder then turned back to the window, her back rigid. In the shiny surface of the glass she could see both their reflections so close together, yet she had never felt more distant from him than she did at that moment. Deep down Kate knew she should make him tell her what was going on, what was troubling him, yet some inner fear stemmed the questions in her throat and kept her silent.

'I'm sorry, Kate.'

Kate turned slowly to face him, unable to bear the tension and uncertainty a second longer.

'Why, Aaron? Why are you sorry? Can't you tell me what's wrong?' Her hand sliced through the air to cut off the denial she could see forming on his lips. 'No, don't lie to me! I know something is wrong. Why won't you tell me what it is?'

'Nothing is wrong, Kate. You're imagining things. I'm sorry because I have to go out, but I'm afraid it's quite unavoidable.'

It was obvious from the brusqueness of his tone that he had no intention of telling her anything further, and Kate bit her lip to stem the mounting wave of hysteria. It was his business where he was going and why, and he couldn't have made it clearer if he'd shouted it at her rather than used that coolly impersonal tone. After all, why should she think that he owed her any explanations just because of a few hours of shared passion?

She stood up straighter, pulling the tattered remnants of dignity round her like a shield.

'Of course. I understand. I'm sorry if you thought I was prying. Where you go and for what reason is none of my business, is it?'

'Dammit, Kate, that wasn't what I meant at all! Look, it's not too late yet. I can cancel my plans and stay here with——'

'No! No, please don't do that on my account. I shall be fine. When will you be back?'

'I don't know yet. A few hours, possibly longer. It's hard to say at present.'

He walked over to the desk and picked up the case, then hesitated as though undecided what to do next, and suddenly Kate knew she didn't want him to stay on her account . . . out of pity!

'Right. Well, I'd better go and get dressed, then. I've a few things to do before I go to visit Chrissie. I'll see you later, whenever you get back.'

She went to walk past him but he dropped the case and caught her arm, swinging her round so that her body fell heavily against his. For a second he stared deep into her eyes, then bent his head and took her mouth in a brief, fierce kiss which left her reeling.

'Goodbye, Kate. Take care. Remember that I only ever wanted what was right . . . that I never meant to hurt you.'

He let her go and picked up the case, striding from the room and out of the house before Kate could draw enough breath to ask him what he meant by that strangely evocative statement. Lifting her hand, she pressed a trembling finger to her mouth, desperately trying to keep the warmth of his kiss on her lips, but slowly it faded. Tears filled her eyes and impatiently she blinked them away. Why on earth was she crying? Because Aaron had left her? That was ridiculous. He'd told her he would be back later, so what was she doing standing here snivelling?

Chiding herself for being stupid, Kate hurried back upstairs to shower and dress, but it seemed impossible to rid herself of the feeling of abandonment, the idea that Aaron really had left her.

CHAPTER NINE

IT WAS late when Jack dropped Kate off after her hospital visit. She stood on the step to wave to him, her eyes holding a hint of puzzlement as she watched him drive away.

What had been the matter with him today? He had seemed so tense, so distracted, barely hearing a word either she or Chrissie had said to him. She could understand him still being upset about the burglary, yet she'd had the strangest feeling that there had been something else troubling him apart from that. When she had rung him earlier in the day, offering her help to tidy up the flat, he had been uncharacteristically sharp with her, almost rude in his swift refusal of the offer. Kate had felt both hurt and annoyed that he should speak to her that way, and if it hadn't been for the fact that she knew he was under pressure from the strain of keeping it all from Chrissie she would have had it out with him on the drive back tonight. Still, maybe that was the explanation for it all; maybe he was missing Chrissie more than he cared to admit ... even to himself!

With a wry little laugh, Kate opened the front door and walked into the house, pausing just inside the doorway, her ears straining for any hint of noise which might mean Aaron had come back, but the house was silent, empty. He'd been gone for hours now. When would he be back?

Pushing the nagging little question to the back of her mind as she had tried to do all day, Kate shrugged off her coat and hung it on the hallstand before walking through to the kitchen and filling the kettle. She made some tea then opened the fridge, her eyes skimming over the well-stocked shelves with little interest. She had eaten nothing all day apart from a slice of toast in the hospital canteen, yet she didn't feel hungry. Perhaps she would wait until Aaron got back and then make them both something. It would give her something to look forward to, the thought of sharing a meal with him at the end of what had turned out to be such an unsettling day.

Too restless to sit at the small pine table in the kitchen, Kate carried the cup with her as she wandered aimlessly round the house, peering into the silent, empty rooms. She stopped outside the study, her mind flashing back to what had happened there just hours ago before she determinedly pushed the thoughts away. She wouldn't let herself go looking for trouble like that, go dredging up problems where there might be none. If Aaron had acted strangely then it had been because he was worried about some sort of business problem, and had nothing at all to do with her. She would be better advised to focus her thoughts on what had happened before that, on those magical hours they had spent together. She could build a lifetime on memories as wonderful as those.

Comforted by the magic of those memories, Kate started back to the kitchen, then stopped as she caught sight of the jumble of files still lying untidily on the desk. Aaron had been in such a hurry to leave that morning that he hadn't stopped to clear them away. She couldn't leave the room looking like this for him to come home to. He would be tired after all these hours sorting out whatever the problem was and wouldn't feel like tackling this mess. What was to stop her from clearing up the files and putting them back in the cabinet? It would mean he would have more time for important things, like *her*, when he got back!

Setting the cup down on to the leather blotter, Kate gathered up the scattered folders, her hands moving swiftly and deftly as she ran them back into order. She opened the top drawer of the tall metal filing cabinet and ran an assessing glance along the row of neatly labelled files, smiling when she realised they were arranged in a simple alphabetical order which should pose no problem for her. Quickly and efficiently she slid them back into place, working her way down the drawers, following the orderly sequence. It was obvious from the way they were arranged that Aaron was particular about keeping everything in perfect order, and Kate took care to ensure that nothing was put back in the wrong place.

She opened the last drawer and worked her way through it, her nimble fingers separating the buff-coloured folders as she muttered the names neatly printed on their tags under her breath.

'Walker, A. Walsh, T. Walters, B. Warren, K. West——'

She stopped abruptly, her lips freezing into a rigid curve as she realised what name she'd just read on that last file. Surely she must have imagined it, misread the neat, precise lettering. The lighting in the room was poor, and her eyes were getting tired from constantly peering at the small labels.

Excuse after excuse poured through Kate's brain as she stood and stared at the long row of files, but she knew she couldn't accept a single one of them. She had to know without a shadow of a doubt that she'd been wrong, that she hadn't seen her name on that slim manilla wallet.

With leaden fingers she worked her way back along the row, but she was trembling so much that she couldn't seem to find the one she wanted. Resting her forehead against the cold metal frame of the cabinet, Kate drew in a long, steadying breath then tried again, taking her time separating each folder from the next, hoping against hope that she'd been wrong, but she hadn't. With a feeling of cold disbelief, her eyes finally halted on the one name she had never expected to see... her name.

There was a buzzing, roaring sound in her head and Kate stepped back from the cabinet, snatching her hands away from the file as though it had scorched her fingers. The roaring was louder now, filling her head, making her feel dizzy and sick, and she pressed her hands to her ears to stem the heavy, relentless pounding. She had to calm down, had to think, had to decide what to do next, but it seemed impossible as the full enormity of the find overwhelmed her.

Why did Aaron have a file on her? What did it mean? The questions filtered through the roaring, bringing her back from the very edge of faintness, and suddenly Kate knew that she had to look, had to see what was in that file no matter how much the idea terrified her. With shaking hands she pulled it from the drawer, uncaring that several others came out with it, or that they fell on to the floor. All she could focus on was this one file, this single folder, marked with her name.

She walked over to the desk, her movements stiff, jerky, strangely uncoordinated as she tipped its contents on to the smoothly polished surface and watched as the papers slid in a dozen different directions before settling into an untidy heap. One by one, Kate picked them up and looked at them, studying each news cutting, each photograph, each neatly typed sheet, unable to comprehend what she was seeing.

It was all there, every single word that had ever been written about her trial, every photograph that had ever been published, everything about her relationship with Jonathan, plus more, a whole lot more. With a mounting, disbelieving horror, Kate picked up just one of the close-typed reports and scoured the pages, feeling sick to her stomach as she read the intimate details it contained about her life.

Where had Aaron got this information from? How had he found out all these details about the life she'd led before she even met Jonathan Knight? None of this had been made public at the trial. No one had ever wanted to know where she had gone to school or what her favourite colour was, so how had Aaron Blake accumulated all this information? He had discovered the most intimate details about her, laid bare her soul, but why? What did it all mean?

Kate didn't know, couldn't even begin to understand his reasons for compiling this dossier on her. All she knew, with a deep-seated conviction, was that she had to get away from this whole nightmare situation now. She ran from the room and across the hall, snatching her coat from the stand with such force that the lining ripped. She dragged it on then picked up her bag, crying out in dismay as it fell from her shaking hands and scattered its contents across the floor. Kate bent down and gathered them up, stuffing lipsticks and comb and coins back into the leather bag with scant regard for any kind of order, one thought and one alone echoing round her head. She had to get away, now... before Aaron came back!

The doorbell rang so suddenly that Kate reeled back against the wall, the last vestige of colour draining from her face. She clamped a hand over her mouth, biting hard on the soft flesh as she tried to hold back the scream forming in her throat. With wild, frightened eyes she stared at the door, cringing back against the wall as it rang again, and then again, echoing time after time around the silent hall. Whoever was ringing that bell was doing so with a certainty and conviction that it would be answered, yet who apart from Aaron and Jack knew she was here? Could she really risk opening the door and finding the man she was trying to avoid waiting out on the step?

'Come on, Katie. Open up. I know you're in there.'

The voice was familiar, so familiar that Kate felt herself swaying as the second part of the nightmare unfolded around her.

'Dammit, Katie! Open up, do you hear?'

There was no way she could ignore the summons, no way she could hide and hope he would go away. Deep down she had always known that he would find her, some time, some place, somewhere. On leaden legs she walked to the door and opened it, a strange calmness governing her actions as she stared at the man standing on the step. His face was in shadow, the collar of his coat turned up, the brim of a hat pulled low, but she had no difficulty in recognising him.

'Hello, Katie. Surprised to see me?'

How many times had she heard that voice and felt the blood race hotly through her veins as he said her name in that very way? Kate didn't know, but there was no heat inside her now, no warmth, just the cold slither of ice sliding inexorably through her body.

She'd had no answers yet, no explanations as to why that file was in Aaron's possession, yet suddenly Kate knew with a chilling certainty that it had something and everything to do with the man standing on the step. She clung hold of the door, her fingers gripping it tightly, needing its solidity to hang on to as the world crumbled around her.

'What do you want, Jonathan?' she asked, her voice a mere whisper of sound against the night's stillness. 'Why have you come?'

He pushed past her, sweeping off his hat before turning in a slow circle as he ran an assessing glance around the hall. He turned back to Kate, his face holding little warmth as he smiled coldly at her.

'Why do I get the impression that you're not pleased to see me, Katie? That is disappointing. I had hoped that you would be as eager to pick up where we left off as I am.'

'Pick up where...?' Temper rippled through her and Kate pushed the door to before turning to confront him. In the overhead light her face was pale, her skin gleaming with a pearlised translucence intensified by the hectic glitter of her green eyes. 'How dare you come here and tell me that you expect to pick up where we left off? You might have forgotten about the trial, about the way you used me and made me a scapegoat for your rotten filthy deals, but I haven't! There are words for men like you, Jonathan, but I won't soil my lips by repeating them. Now get out of here before I call the police. As far as I know that warrant for your arrest still holds good, doesn't it?'

She brushed past him, her hand reaching for the telephone resting on the hall table, but he was there before her. Picking it up, he wrenched it from its socket and flung it across the hall so hard that it smashed against the wall. Kate stepped back a pace, her eyes wary as she saw the uncontrollable fury on his face and the way his pale eyes were glittering dangerously. Suddenly she was afraid, afraid of what this man might do to her if he was crossed.

'Don't threaten me, Katie,' he said quietly, his voice a low purr of menace which made her heart pound wildly in fear. 'I don't like people threatening me. Now, how about us sitting down and having a drink and a nice cosy little chat while I explain exactly why I'm here?'

He caught hold of her arm, his fingers biting cruelly into the soft flesh as he hauled her along beside him, and Kate bit her lip to stem the protests. Jonathan had always been quick-tempered; on more than one occasion she had seen him tear an employee off a strip for some quite trivial misdemeanour, but now there was a depth to his anger which bordered on the manic. Suddenly, Kate knew that the only way she was going to get herself out of this mess was by treading carefully and pretending to go along with him.

She pulled her arm free and summoned up a smile. 'All right, Jonathan. That's fine by me. Come in here and we can sit down and talk, and have that drink you mentioned. I was just surprised to see you, and hurt, of course, about the way you seemingly deserted me.'

Would he believe her? Holding her breath, Kate led the way into the sitting-room and poured him a glass of whisky, praying that he would accept her explanation for her anger. With the phone well and truly out of action now, and no one else in the house to help her, she was in a very vulnerable position if he turned nasty.

A heavy brooding silence filled the room and Kate felt her nerves stretching to their limits as she waited. Then he spoke, his voice once more smoothly complacent.

'All that is in the past now, Katie. What is important is that I've come back to see you.'

Well, no one on God's green earth could ever accuse the man of having an underdeveloped ego, could they?

Kate swallowed down a few spiky comments, waiting silently as he settled himself comfortably on the sofa before handing him the drink. She poured herself a small measure of the whisky, then sat down opposite him and took a tiny sip. Although she desperately needed the boost it could give her sagging courage, the very last thing she must do was to let herself get tipsy. She sat back in the chair and crossed her legs, holding back the swift revulsion which welled inside her as she saw the way Jonathan's eyes followed the movement and lingered on their slender length. She couldn't afford to let her feelings show and antagonise him again when he was in this highly volatile state. She had to keep things cool and calm while she found out what it was he wanted from her.

'How did you manage to slip back into the country, Jonathan? According to the last report I read you were somewhere in America.'

He shrugged, taking a long swallow of the whisky before he answered. 'It's easy enough if you have the right connections which, fortunately, I still have.'

'But wasn't it a risk? I mean, anyone could have recognised you, especially here in London where you're so well known. Aren't you afraid that someone will spot you and call the police?'

He laughed, a mocking, triumphant sound which made Kate grind her teeth together.

'Recognise me . . . no, I don't think so. After all, you didn't recognise me the other night, did you, Katie?'

'Me? But where...when?' The shivers were dancing up and down her spine now and Kate put the glass down, frightened he would see how her hand was shaking as she held it.

'Outside the casino. I was on the corner when you drove past the other night. You stared right at me, Katie, and for a moment I did wonder if you had recognised me, but obviously not.'

'That was you! I had the feeling that I knew... but...' Words failed her for a moment as she remembered the strange feeling she'd had when she'd spotted that lone figure. How could she have been so close and yet failed to recognise him?

'Yes, that was me, and me in the alley too. I must admit I was rather disappointed when I first realised it was you huddled in that gateway looking like a drowned rat. However, when I saw you drive past in that car...well, that soon changed my mind, I can tell you, Katie.' He glanced round the room, his face expressive as he studied the expensive décor. 'Yes, indeed, it looks like you've well and truly landed on your feet here. Clever girl. Somehow I never expected you to have an eye to the main chance like this, but I admire you for it.'

Kate's face flamed as she realised what he was implying, but she stayed silent. Clasping her hands tightly together in her lap, she strove to stay calm and make sense of the real reason behind Jonathan's visit. He had never bothered to enquire if there was anyone else in the house with her before he pushed his way inside so obviously he must have been watching her, monitoring her movements and Aaron's to find a time when she was alone. Yet why had he come? Why had he run the risk of being apprehended by returning to the country? Suddenly Kate knew she had to find out the reason for it.

'Why have you come back, Jonathan, and why did you run such a risk of being spotted by going to the casino? Did you come back to see Jack?'

'See my dear, adopted brother? No, Katie, the only place I'd like to see him is in hell, where he belongs!'

He slammed the glass down on to the table and Kate winced as it scored heavily into the polished surface, gouging a deep groove out of the wood. She had always known that there was no love lost between Jonathan and Jack, but she had never realised before just how much he hated the older man. Thank heavens they hadn't met up the other night, because she had the horrible feeling that the outcome of such a meeting could be devastating.

'Still, I think I gave my dear brother a few things to think about when he got home the other night ... Yes, more than a few.'

His low chuckle drew her abruptly back to the present and she glanced towards him, her eyes holding a question.

'What do you mean?'

'Surely you've heard about the burglary, sweetheart? You must have! I made such a good job of it. There was hardly a stick of furniture intact by the time I'd finished.'

'It was you! You who broke into the flat? But why? Are you crazy?'

His face went livid with anger at the question, and Kate shrank back in her seat as he half rose, before changing his mind and picking up the glass again. He drained the whisky then smiled coldly at her.

'No, I'm not crazy, Katie, but I'm sure that brother of mine must have felt a bit like that for the past couple of days. I took the liberty of leaving a few— how shall I put it—a few poignant messages on the walls which should give him something to worry about. Serves him right. If it hadn't been for him then none of this would ever have happened. That casino and the rest should have been mine, all of it. Father had no right to hand it over to him and put him in charge of the purse strings. I am his real son, not Jack!'

There was a note of rising hysteria in his voice which made Kate's stomach lurch when she heard it. In a sudden flash she remembered all that Chrissie had told her, about the rivalry which had always existed between the two brothers. Jack had been adopted by the Knights just a couple of years before they had conceived a child of their own, Jonathan. Jonathan had always felt that his adopted brother had usurped his rightful place and stolen his inheritance. When she had been dating him, Kate had always felt a certain sympathy with him, yet now, hearing that note in his voice, that bitter hint of madness, she knew she'd been wrong. There was something unstable about Jonathan Knight which his parents must have recognised. What had been in those messages he'd left painted on the walls, what sort of sick threats? Suddenly, Kate was glad that she hadn't seen the outpourings of his hatred.

'So you came back to get even with Jack, is that it?' she asked quietly, anxious to keep him talking, to keep his mind off whatever it was that made his face look like a mask of evil hatred.

For a moment she thought she hadn't succeeded, but then he shrugged, standing up to pour himself another measure of the whisky.

'Not really. That was just a bonus. I came back because there is something in the flat that I need.'

'And what's that?'

'The key to a safety deposit box.' He took a long swallow, then wiped his mouth on the back of his hand and smiled at her. Kate was disturbed to see the rim of colour which edged his cheekbones and the glitter of excitement burning in his eyes as he studied her thoughtfully.

'You see, Katie, it costs money to stay hidden from the law in any degree of comfort and I've almost used up everything I had in the States. Fortunately, I took the precaution of creaming off some of my...earnings, and depositing them here. Now I've come back to reclaim them, and that's where you come in, my sweet.'

'Me? What can I do?' Her voice was shrill and she swallowed hard to ease the tension knotting her throat.

'You can get me the key. I couldn't find it the other night. Everything has been moved round so that I couldn't find the ornament I'd hidden it in, but you can find it for me. After all, Jack married your sister. You must have free access to that place.'

'But how can I? I don't know which ornament you've hidden it in and I can't just go rooting round the whole flat. Jack would know there was something going on. Be sensible, Jonathan.'

'No, you be sensible, Katie. I need that key, I need that money, and you are going to get it for me!'

'And if I refuse?'

'Then I shall be forced to tell a few tales to your friend who owns this rather sumptuous house. Does he know what happened, Katie? Does he know you went on trial for drug smuggling? I'm sure he doesn't. You went to a lot of trouble, hiding yourself away in the depths of Liverpool, making sure that no one found out about your past. No, I'm almost certain he doesn't know.'

A couple of hours back, Kate knew she would almost have been tempted to agree to his demands just to stop him telling Aaron everything about her. Now, however, the bitter irony of it all nearly choked her. She stood up and walked stiffly from the room, hearing the soft tread of footsteps as Jonathan followed her into the study. The lights were still switched on and she saw his expression alter as he spotted the heap of cuttings and photos strewn across the desk. Silently, she waved a hand towards them, watching with a cold indifference as he worked through the pile before tossing the last one into the empty grate with a snarl of anger.

'So much for your threats, Jonathan,' she said softly. 'I doubt if there's much you can tell Aaron about me apart from what brand of toothpaste I prefer, do you?'

'Where did he get all this?'

There was tension in his voice now, a fleeting hint of . . . what on his face? Fear? Kate didn't know, and frankly didn't care. All she wanted was for him to leave so that she could close the last chapter on the book.

'I don't know, but what does it matter where or how? As far as I'm concerned you can tell whoever you want because I've had enough of both you and the whole rotten business! It's over, Jonathan, all over.'

'Oh, no, it's not, Katie. That's where you're wrong. It won't be over till I get my money . . . until you get it for me!'

With a sudden turn of speed he pulled her roughly into his arms, holding her so tightly that she could hardly breathe. 'Think of it, Katie, all those hundreds of thousands of pounds. More money than you can imagine, all for us to spend on having a good time. It would be marvellous, Katie, just you and me, if you'll help me get it back.'

'No! I don't want your filthy money, don't want to share anything with you! You make me sick, Jonathan Knight, sick . . . sick . . . sick! Now let me go.'

She twisted round, desperately trying to free herself, but he clamped a hand to the back of her head, his eyes glittering with fury.

'Make you sick, do I? Since when? I never used to make you sick, *darling*! Oh, you put on a good act, played the reluctant little virgin, but I could have had you any time I'd wanted!'

He bent his head, his mouth fastening to hers with a harsh brutality which brought tears to her eyes. Kate tried to turn her head away, moaning in fear and pain as she tried to drag her mouth away from the bruising pressure, but he was too strong for her. In desperation, she raised her hand and scored her nails down the side of his cheek, and felt him jerk back in pain as she drew blood.

'Why, you little——!'

A murderous rage twisted his face now, and Kate cried out in alarm as his fingers curled round her throat.

'Let her go!'

She hadn't heard him come in, hadn't heard the sound of a door opening or the brush of a footstep, and now she went weak with relief as she recognised Aaron's voice. As Jonathan relaxed his grip on her she stepped smartly back, moving several yards away from him before turning to look at the man standing just inside the room. He wasn't looking at her though, his attention was all focused on Jonathan who was standing white-faced and silent, and suddenly Kate knew that this was what it had all been leading to: this confrontation between the two men.

'Now look, it's not what you think.'

There was a hunted look on Jonathan's face which Kate could well appreciate. Although Aaron hadn't moved a muscle yet, or said anything apart from that one brief order, there was a coiled tension about him, a readiness which hinted at danger. Just standing silently at the door he seemed to dominate the whole room.

'Isn't it?'

His voice was low, cool, and Jonathan evidently took heart from the reasonable tone.

'No. Katie and I are old friends. I was just kissing her as a kind of "hello". There was nothing in it, old chap. Nothing for you to get upset about.'

Kate nearly gagged on the suppressed bitter laughter welling in her throat as she realised that even now Jonathan hadn't fully grasped the implications of the situation. He seemed to think that Aaron was merely jealous, but was he wrong! It wasn't jealousy which turned Aaron's face into a harsh, cold mask, not jealousy which gave his eyes that glitter, but a deep, burning hatred which made her stomach clench in apprehension. At that moment Kate would have given anything to be able to run from the room and leave them to it, but she couldn't: not yet, not till it was all finally over.

'No?'

'No, of course not. Look, it's getting late, so don't you think it would be better if I left? I'm sure Katie can explain everything to you far better than I can.'

Jonathan smiled shakily and took a step towards the door, coming to a halt when Aaron made no move to step out of his way.

'Of course you mustn't go yet. Stay and have a little chat. I'm sure you'll find we have a lot in common.'

How could anyone inject such simple words with so much menace? Kate didn't know, but she felt the shiver which rippled through her as a mirror image of the one which ran through Jonathan. It was like watching a panther stalk its prey, watching Aaron play with the other man this way.

'Well, that is kind of you, Mr—er—but I really think I should——'

'Sit down, Knight. You're not going anywhere, not until I say so.'

'You know who I am?'

Nonplussed, Jonathan sat down heavily on a nearby chair, his face paling to a sickly grey hue as he stared at the dark-haired man, and Kate could almost sympathise with him. She walked slowly across the room and sat down too, knowing her knees were in danger of giving way on her. She could feel Aaron watching her, but she didn't look at him. It was over between them, and now all she wanted to do was find out why he'd planned all this before she left for good. The thought made her heart ache.

'Yes, I know your name, know all about you, in fact. I've made it my business to find out, but do you know why?'

Kate looked at him then, seeing the way he stood with his hands pushed easily into the pockets of his trousers. He looked relaxed, yet Kate could feel the tension oozing from him and knew that Jonathan could feel it too. Aaron Blake was rapidly approaching the kill.

Jonathan shook his head, his eyes sliding this way and that as he searched for a way out, but with Aaron guarding the doorway there was none.

'No? Well, perhaps my name means something to you. It's Blake, Aaron Blake. Does that ring a bell? No, I can see it doesn't, but how about Sarah Blake?

Surely you remember her, don't you? Sweet little Sarah who was only seventeen when you met her. Let me show you a photograph to jog your memory.'

He pulled his wallet from his pocket and tossed a plastic-covered photograph across the room, but Jonathan made no attempt to catch it as it fluttered to the floor. Kate stared at it, studying the delicate features of the pretty dark-haired girl who bore such a striking resemblance to Aaron. Who was she?

'Remember her now, do you? Remember pretty, bright little Sarah? Remember how she was, and what she was like after you'd started her on your filthy drugs? Surely you must remember how she died. It made the headlines, Sarah's own four minutes of fame when she threw herself off the top of that building, her body so full of your filthy merchandise that she thought she could fly. Remember now, Knight? Remember Sarah, my sister!'

There was a bitter anger in Aaron's voice, a haunting anguish which brought tears to Kate's eyes as she heard it. She looked down again at the photograph, seeing the sweetly delicate features, the innocence in the girl's dark eyes: seeing the real reason why Aaron had sought her out.

'Kate.'

He spoke her name softly and she looked up, her eyes swimming with unshed tears as they met his for a brief moment before she lowered them back to the photograph. Oh, she could understand what had driven him to do it, but she couldn't forgive him, couldn't forget that he had been prepared to do anything to achieve his objective—even make her fall in love with him. That had been just too cruel for her to ever forgive.

'Kate,' he repeated, his voice strangely gentle after the harsh way he had spoken to the man still cowering silently in the chair. 'Will you go out to the car, please, and telephone the police? I want this finished, here and now, before any more lives are ruined.'

Kate nodded, not trusting herself to speak in case she broke down completely. She walked from the room, not glancing at either man as she left. In their own way both had used her, yet the pain she had once felt over Jonathan's deception paled to insignificance compared with what she felt now because of Aaron's.

'I'm sorry, Kate.'

The whispered apology followed her from the room, but she didn't stop, didn't even pause to look back. It was over now, everything, every single foolish dream lying shattered and broken. She never wanted to see Aaron Blake again.

CHAPTER TEN

THE river slid past, its grey waters reflecting the leaden weight of the sky and mirroring the heaviness which filled her heart.

Kate stared out across the broad expanse of water, scarcely feeling the icy wind which chafed her skin and blew her hair back from her face. A sleeting rain was falling, settling coldly on to her head and shoulders, but she was as oblivious to its stinging touch as she was to the sounds of voices and roar of traffic. In this city of thousands she stood alone, with just the river and the never-ending ache which filled her heart for company.

It was six weeks since she had last seen Aaron, six weeks since she'd walked out of his house that night with her life in tatters, and the pain she'd felt then hadn't dimmed one little bit. Time was supposedly a great healer, yet each day seemed harder to bear than the one before, each night more agonising than the previous. She loved him, and that love was tearing her apart.

With a sigh Kate turned away from the river and made her way towards the hotel, shivering slightly as she suddenly realised just how cold and wet she felt. She glanced at her watch, then quickened her pace as she discovered it was just three minutes short of the hour. Jack might have given her this job in one of his hotel restaurants, but it was up to her to keep it, and being late for work definitely wouldn't help! His plan, that she should train in every aspect of restaurant work and then take up a management position with his company, was the only thing which had kept her going these past weeks. It was something to aim for, a plan for the future; the one hope she had to cling to that some day life would be worth living.

The lunchtime flew past. Kate took orders, served meals and cleared tables, smiling until her face ached from the effort. Several times she was aware of people watching her, but she ignored the curious glances and carried on with her duties with a calm aloofness which quelled any comments. Jonathan's arrest and all the subsequent publicity had brought her back into the public eye with a vengeance, but she had learned to live with it this time, to ignore all the veiled looks and whispered comments. Compared with the pain she felt over Aaron's deception, it meant nothing.

'Phew! It's busy today, isn't it? I sometimes wonder if there's anyone left in this whole city who knows how to cook a meal for themselves!'

Lisa, one of the other waitresses, stopped beside Kate, her face wry as she eased her aching feet out of her shoes for a moment. Kate smiled sympathetically back at her, silently agreeing that waitressing could be very hard on the feet.

'It certainly is. I don't think I've ever seen the place so full on a lunchtime. Just that one table of mine over in the corner empty.'

'Number fourteen? Yes, and even that's got a reservation on it. Must be someone pretty special if old Graham's prepared to keep it free. I've seen him turn several people away as it is.'

Kate glanced back at the table, her eyes lingering on the pristine freshness of the pale pink cloth, the crisp lines of the single untouched napkin, wondering who the VIP could be. As Lisa had said, it must be someone very special if the head waiter was prepared to turn away business just to hold the table for him.

'Well, well, I wonder if that's your missing customer. Mmm...definitely worth waiting for, if you want my opinion.'

There was open admiration in Lisa's voice and Kate turned quickly to see who had earned such an appreciative comment. For one long, dreadful moment she stared at the tall figure standing just inside the doorway, feeling every single drop of blood drain from her face. She caught hold of a nearby chair and hung on grimly as the room started to tilt and slide out of focus.

'Kate! What's the matter? Kate!'

Lisa shook her arm, her voice urgent as she saw Kate's pallor, and Kate tried desperately to control the feeling that the floor was rushing up to meet her. She closed her eyes, forcing herself to breathe slowly and deeply, to rid herself of the momentary madness. It had been a trick of the light, that was all, a fleeting hallucination brought on by the strain she'd been living under for the past few weeks. It wasn't Aaron standing in that doorway...it couldn't be!

Reluctantly, she opened her eyes again and looked back at the doorway, her heart leaping wildly as she met his eyes across the width of the room.

'No! No!'

She didn't realise that she had cried the denial aloud until a hush fell over the room. Glancing round, Kate suddenly discovered everyone was watching her with open curiosity. Colour surged back to her face and she swung round, turning her back on all the avid glances.

Why had he come? What did he want? It couldn't be mere coincidence which had brought Aaron to this very restaurant where she worked, yet what right did he have to come here and embarrass her after what he'd done? She owed him nothing now, no thanks, no debts...nothing! He'd had his reward in finding Jonathan, so what did he think he was doing seeking her out and making a show of her?

The first ripple of anger flowed through her, followed by a second, and then a third, until a huge great tidal wave was building up inside her. She snatched up a menu, her face filled with a fury which made Lisa take a hasty step backwards and swallow her offer to attend to the client now seated at table fourteen. In open-mouthed horror she could only watch as Kate strode across the room and slapped the menu down on the table with a force which made the glasses rattle and the cutlery clatter, wondering what on earth was going on.

'Your menu, sir.'

Her voice was cold, so cold that every word seemed to hang in the air like a verbal icicle. Aaron glanced down at the menu but made no move to open it before he looked up at her. Kate had to steel herself as she felt his eyes trace over her face in a slow, assessing glance which seemed to strip her bare.

'How have you been, Kate?' he asked softly, his voice so deep and seductively intimate that it seemed to cut them off from the noisy chatter in the rest of the room, but Kate wasn't going to fall for that sort of tactic!

She glared at him, her face set, her mouth drawn into a mutinous curl. 'Fine, thank you, *sir*! Would you like to order a drink before lunch?'

Picking up the neat little notebook attached to the leather belt round her trim waist, she stood with pencil poised to take the order. There was silence, a heavy brooding silence, and she slanted a mocking eyebrow at him when he didn't answer.

'I take it that you don't want a drink, then, sir. Shall I take your order now, or would you prefer me to come back in a few minutes when you've had time to inspect the menu?'

'Dammit, Kate, I didn't come here to order lunch, and well you know it!'

Impatience bristled through the deep tones now, and Kate felt a flicker of satisfaction rise inside her as she realised that she had managed to prick his composure. She smiled calmly back at him, studying the scowl which darkened his brow and pulled the corners of his mouth down. If she had her way then Aaron Blake would rue the day he had ever decided to reserve a table here!

'Not order lunch...I'm sorry, sir, but I don't understand. If there's a problem then I can call our head waiter over to help you.'

With a mocking courtesy she half turned to go, stopping abruptly as Aaron caught her wrist, his fingers tightening painfully round the fragile bones.

'I don't know what sort of a game you're playing, Kate,' he growled, glaring at her. 'But we'll play it your way for now, at least. What do you recommend?'

Kate pulled her arm free and picked up the menu, fighting back the sudden weakness which assailed her. She wouldn't let him get to her again, wouldn't allow the touch of his hand against her arm to affect her. Aaron Blake had used her once, and she had to remember that and not allow these foolish, traitorous feelings to make her forget.

'All our dishes are to be recommended, sir,' she said politely, pleased to hear how calm she sounded, and opened the menu for his inspection.

'So, recommend one.'

He leant back in his chair, arms folded across his chest, his face impassive as he stared up at her, and Kate swallowed down a rising tide of panic. She must have read the menu a hundred times in the past few weeks, but for the life of her she couldn't remember a single dish on offer!

She bent down, spreading the menu on the table as she peered at the seething sea of letters, the capitals and commas which wouldn't stay still long enough for her to focus on them, and heard him draw in a sharp breath as her hair brushed against his cheek.

'Kate!'

Her name whispered from him, a tiny sound of aching feeling which shocked her rigid with its intensity. Kate sprang back, snatching up the menu and holding it in front of her like a shield, suddenly terrified of what he might say next.

'Snails,' she said quickly, stuttering out the first thing which came to mind. 'Yes, snails... they... they're our chef's speciality. I'm sure you'll enjoy them. With garlic butter, of course, though you can——'

'I couldn't give a damn if they came with custard, Kate! Why on earth are we going through with this charade? I came here today because I wanted to speak to you, so why don't we cut out all this stupid pretence?'

Just like that! He wanted to speak with her! Never mind what he had done or how he had treated her, he wanted to speak to her and she was expected to quietly fall in with his plans. Like hell she would!

Stepping back from the table, Kate glared at him, her eyes sparkling with a resurgence of her previous anger.

'There is nothing, absolutely *nothing*, that I want to speak to you about. Why don't you leave and save me some time and yourself some money?'

Aaron's eyes narrowed as he studied her angry face and rigid posture, then he smiled, a slow, provocative smile which made her blood boil even higher.

'Leave? Before I've sampled this delicious meal you've so kindly recommended? Why, I couldn't do that, Kate, I really couldn't. I shall stay and see if the chef is really as good as you claim.'

Kate bit her lip to hold back the dozens of caustic comments fighting to get out, hating the way he could make her feel so angry, hating the way he could make

her feel! She swung round and marched towards the
kitchen, temper keeping her company every step of
the way. When she thought of what he had done, and
how he now calmly expected her to fall in with his
plans, she could have screamed. If only she could
teach that infuriating man a lesson, and one he would
never forget.

Thrusting open the swing doors, Kate snatched up
a plate and slid half a dozen snails on to it before
reaching for the garlic butter in is copper pan, then
stopped. For a moment she stared down at the melted
butter, swirling it round and round in a tiny whirlpool,
then slowly, deliberately set it aside. With a nasty little
smile on her lips she picked up a nearby ladle and
poured a large scoopful of golden liquid into a deep
puddle right in the middle of the plate.

'*Mon Dieu!* Kate! But look what you have done,
chérie. Kate . . . Kate!'

The chef's wail of anguish followed her out of the
kitchen and echoed in her wake as she walked calmly
back across the restaurant. She could feel people
watching her, setting their knives and forks aside as
they turned to follow her progress, but she ignored
them. Her eyes were focused on the downbent head
of the dark-haired man sitting at table fourteen. He
was calmly reading the menu now, his attention
centred on its pages so that he wasn't aware of her
arrival until she stopped beside him.

'Your starter, sir. Snails . . . and custard, as you
ordered!'

Startled, Aaron looked up, his eyes widening as Kate
held the plate aloft and quite deliberately tipped its

contents over his head, watching silently as streams of sticky yellow custard slithered down his face and neck.

'Chef's special, sir,' she said, calmly putting the plate down on the table before studying the puddles fast forming in his lap. 'I do hope you enjoy it.'

There was silence in the restaurant, a massive, breathless silence, then pandemonium broke out. From a dozen different directions waiters appeared as if by magic, clutching napkins as they headed towards Aaron, who was still sitting in bemused disbelief. Sedately, Kate walked away from the table, pulling off her cap and tossing it over her shoulder as she made her way to the exit. Behind her she could hear the head waiter calling her name, but she never even spared him a glance. What was the point of going back and letting him rant and rave at her before he sacked her? No, that was it, another job gone, but as far as she was concerned it had been worth it just to pay that arrogant man back! Maybe she would regret what she'd done later, rue the impulse and flash of temper which had cost her a job, but right at that moment she didn't regret a thing!

The rain had stopped when she left the hotel after collecting her things, but the pavements still glistened wetly. Kate paused for a moment to pull the collar of her coat up round her neck to ward off the chilly wind. A taxi drew up at the end of the drive to drop off a fare, and after a moment's hesitation she hurried towards it. Taxis were a luxury she could ill afford, especially today now she was out of work, but why shouldn't she treat herself just this once? Today was a day to remember, surely, so why not round it off in a truly memorable fashion?

'Come back here!'

The angry order stopped her dead in her tracks. With widened eyes Kate glanced over her shoulder, then took to her heels as she caught sight of the man hurrying after her. She climbed into the cab and gabbled her address to the driver, praying he would have enough time to pull out before Aaron caught them up, but it seemed her prayers fell on deaf ears. Wrenching the door open, he climbed in beside her, and Kate shrank back in her seat as she saw the expression on his face.

'Get out,' she ordered, hating the way her voice quavered. 'Get out of here, Aaron Blake! This is my taxi and I'm not sharing it with you or anyone. Get out!'

'Make me, sweetheart. Go on, make me get out.'

He sat back in the seat, his face set into grim lines which made Kate's insides wobble with apprehension. His hair was clean of the sticky mess, lying wetly against his head, but his suit still bore the unmistakable evidence of her actions. Huge greasy stains marred the pale grey wool of his jacket and patched the fabric stretched across his muscular thighs. Kate swallowed when she realised what a dreadful mess she had made of his clothing, then determinedly rallied herself again.

After all, it was his fault for coming to the restaurant in the first place. What they had shared was over now, lying dead and broken because of the way he had deceived her. The thought steadied her, gave her the strength to face him and ignore the heavy, painful pounding of her heart.

'I have no intention of making you do anything, Aaron. What you do is your business, and if you won't get out of this taxi then it seems that I shall have to because there is no way I am going to share it with you.'

She opened the door to climb out but he caught her arm and hauled her back inside.

'No way, lady! There is no way you are going to get away from me after what you've just done. Now sit there and shut up if you've got one grain of sense in your head.'

'Sit there and...now look here, you bully. Just who do you think you are giving me orders? What right do you have to tell me what to do?'

'What right...what right? I'll tell you what right I have. I love you, and that gives me all the rights in the world!'

'You love me!' For a moment Kate could only echo his words, her eyes huge and startled, her whole body trembling. Suddenly the anger drained from his face and he leant over to cup her cheek gently.

'I love you, Kate. I've fought against it, believe me, tried to convince myself that what I feel for you is anything but love, but there's no way I can keep on pretending. I know I've hurt you but, please, believe me when I say that I shall never hurt you again. I asked you once to trust me, and I know it's a lot to ask you to do it again, but will you? Will you trust me one more time and give me a chance to explain?'

The question hung in the air, gentle, waiting, and Kate turned away as tears misted her eyes. Could she do it? Could she risk even more pain by trusting him again?

'Please, Kate.'

There was anguish in his voice and on his face as she turned to study its tense lines, and Kate knew she wasn't proof against his pleas.

'Yes,' she whispered. 'Yes, I'll trust you, Aaron, just one more time.'

The house was quiet when they arrived. Aaron led the way into the sitting-room and Kate followed slowly. She looked round, remembering with a sudden vivid clarity what had happened there the last time. A shiver raced through her body and she wrapped her arms tightly round herself to quell the tremor. Aaron must have noticed, however, because he came towards her, but Kate eluded him as he tried to take her into his arms. She wanted to hear what he had to say first, to listen to his explanations and not be swayed by the longings of her body.

She sat down on the sofa, her hands clasped so tightly in her lap that her fingers started to go numb from the pressure, but she couldn't relax, couldn't give in to the tiny flame of hope flickering hesitantly to life inside her. Maybe later she could let herself believe that this really was the end of the whole nightmare, but not yet.

Aaron sat down opposite her, staring down at the soft swirling patterns on the rug for long minutes before he spoke slowly, as though he found it difficult to find the right words.

'I know nothing can excuse what I did, Kate, but maybe when you've heard the reasons for it you will be able to forgive me.' He glanced up, searching her face, but Kate said nothing because there was nothing she could say. With a sigh he continued, his voice deep and filled with an ache which tore her heart as she heard it.

'Sarah, my sister, was much younger than me. She was born just a few months before Dad died and seemed to be doubly precious because of that. When we were young money was scarce, but as I began to make a go of the business things got easier. It was only natural that Mother and I should spoil her a little to make up for all she'd missed out on as a child. I wanted her to have the best: the best education, the best clothes, the best friends!'

There was a bitter sadness in his voice, a sorrow which he must have lived with for a long time, and Kate had to steel herself not to go to him and tell him to forget about all these painful explanations. She couldn't do that. She had to hear it all now, and then, maybe, see if there was a way they could build a new life untainted by the grief of the past.

'Is that how she met Jonathan? Was he one of the friends you mentioned?'

Aaron nodded, standing up to cross to the window as though he found it hard to stay sitting quietly.

'Yes. I was away at the time, in America on business, and no one will ever know how I have blamed myself for being out of the country the one time I should have been here.' He ran a hand through his hair, his face tormented as he glanced at Kate. 'Maybe if I'd been here I could have broken up the friendship and realised sooner that Sarah's erratic behaviour was drug-induced. It was quite deliberate, you see; Knight wanted to get her hooked so that she would become a courier for him and do his dirty work while he sat back and reaped the profits.'

Sickness welled in Kate's stomach and she looked away. Had that been what Jonathan had intended for her too? Had he planned to get her dependent on drugs so that she would do much the same thing for him? She would never know, and maybe it was better that she wouldn't.

'By the time I realised what was happening it was already too late. Sarah was beyond reason, totally committed to Knight. I had her admitted to a clinic, but she signed herself out and went back to him. Then, just days later, before I could even track her down, she took the dose which led to her death. I vowed then that I would find some way of bringing Knight to justice for what he had done. However, just as I was making some headway, your court case broke and he disappeared, leaving behind yet another victim—you, Kate. After the trial I thought about contacting you to see if you could help me, but . . .'

'But you didn't,' she finished quietly. 'Why, Aaron? If you had then none of this might ever have happened!'

There was anguish in her voice and she saw him flinch, but he met her eyes steadily.

'I thought you might still be in love with him, Kate.' He held his hand up to stem the hot denial forming on her lips. 'No, hear me out. At your trial you never said one word against him. Oh, you answered every question that was put to you, but never once did you condemn him for what he'd done. It made me wonder if you were still involved with him.'

'I was in shock. I'd tried so hard to convince myself that it was all a dreadful mistake, that Jonathan would come forward and explain, yet day after day there was no sign of him. It wasn't love which held me silent at the trial, Aaron, just horror and disbelief that I could ever have been so stupid. I felt guilty, as though I really was to blame for bringing that package of drugs into the country!'

Tears slid down her cheeks and impatiently she brushed them away, but more kept on flowing. With a low murmur Aaron went to her, pulling her into his arms as he cradled her against him, and Kate let him hold her this time, needing his strength to fight against the painful memories of the past.

'Don't cry, darling. He isn't worth it, Kate, he really isn't.'

How could a man be so intelligent and yet so stupid? Kate pulled herself free, her whole body rigid as she glared up at him.

'For your information, I am *not* crying over Jonathan. As far as I am concerned he doesn't even exist!'

'Then what are you crying about?' Reaching out, Aaron smoothed a silky strand of red hair off her damp cheek, his fingers lingering against the velvety softness. Kate held herself rigid as a slow, steady fire sprang up in her blood and licked along her veins.

'Everything . . . the whole rotten mess. You went to a lot of trouble finding out all those details about me, yet you couldn't see what was in front of your eyes. Did you really believe that I could still feel anything for Jonathan after I'd slept with you? Did you really know so little about me even then to think that?'

'I was confused, Kate. I know that's a poor excuse, but it's the truth. For months I'd lived with the desire to get even with Knight. I felt certain that if he ever did come back into the country you would be the one person he would contact. Then, when I heard a rumour that he was back, I decided to go to Liverpool and check you out, see if you really were as innocent as had been made out. I had some sort of half-baked idea that I might be able to persuade you to help me!' He laughed, a low, bitter laugh. 'What a fool I was, Kate. The minute I saw you in that café everything started to change, all my carefully laid plans! I hadn't been prepared for how vulnerable you would appear, or for the fact that I would feel this instant desire to protect you. How could I explain what I wanted and rake up the past when you seemed to be trying to re-build your life? From that point on I didn't know if I was batting or bowling! I'd gone to Liverpool more than half convinced that you weren't as innocent as you appeared, yet everything about you said otherwise.'

It explained so much, the strange inner tension she'd always sensed in him, as though he'd been waging some silent battle. Surely she could understand what a turmoil he must have been in, but it still hurt that it should have taken so long for him to be convinced about her.

The pain must have shown on her face because he smoothed a kiss over her lips, his voice husky with regret when he spoke.

'Forgive me, Kate. I know I should have trusted my instincts sooner, but I was terrified I might be making a dreadful mistake. Then, when we got to London everything started to move with such a speed that there was never any real opportunity to talk. Jack had that burglary and told me that he suspected Jonathan was behind it. I had already admitted to him why I'd sought you out and, although he wasn't too keen, he agreed not to say anything to you. I think we both hoped that you would never have to find out that Jonathan was back in the country, but that wasn't to be. That morning, when I received the phone call and left the house so abruptly, it was because I'd been tipped off that Knight was in the vicinity. It was obvious that he had traced you to my house and, although every bit of me wanted to warn you, I just couldn't. It was probably the one and only chance I would ever get of catching him and I couldn't lose it, Kate. I couldn't!'

'So you used me as a decoy, your own little sitting duck!'

Bitter anger laced her voice as she pulled away from him, and a spasm of pain crossed his face as he heard it. He half reached a hand towards her, then let it drop to his side in an oddly defeated gesture.

'I'm not proud of what I did, Kate, but I had to. I couldn't let him escape, no matter how much I hated myself for leaving you like that. It was the last thing I could ever do for Sarah and I had to do it, had to make certain that he would never get the chance to destroy anyone else's life. I love you, Kate. When you walked out that night I tried to make myself believe that it was for the best and that I should let you go, but I couldn't. I need you, Kate, need you to make my life complete again, but can you ever find it in your heart to forgive me?' He smiled, a sad little smile which tugged at her heart-strings and made her ache deep inside for the torment he was suffering. 'There's really nothing more I can say, Kate, than that. I love you and I shall always love you. Is it enough?'

Enough? Was it enough to wipe out all the painful memories? Enough to start afresh and build a new life on? It was... more than enough!

'Yes, Aaron. Yes, it is, because I love you too.'

She smiled at him, her face alight with love and happiness, and heard him gasp her name. He took a step towards her, cursing loudly as the telephone rang.

'That damned phone! I swear I'll have it disconnected.'

Kate chuckled softly as she watched him stride impatiently out of the room, and hugged her arms tightly round her body to hold on to the delicious feeling of happiness. She felt greedy for it, desperate not to spill a single drop of the joy which was fast replacing all the pain and heartache. 'I love you, Kate.' They were the most beautiful and precious words she had ever heard.

'That was Jack. Someone at the restaurant told him what had happened, so he rightly guessed you might be here.'

Aaron came back into the room, his blue eyes filled with laughter as he took her into his arms. Kate snuggled against him, burrowing her face into the warm, hard curve of his shoulder, loving the feel of his body against hers. The happiness seemed to be addling her brain, making it difficult to think, so that all she could manage was a faint murmur.

'Mmm?'

Aaron feathered a kiss across her brow, his lips sliding deliciously warm over her skin, making her shiver with pleasure.

'Jack . . . you know, Chrissie's husband?'

There was a teasing note in his voice, and Kate smiled before suddenly appreciating the implications of the statement. She eased a few inches of space between their bodies so that she could try to think straight, but Aaron only pulled her back.

'Was he very angry about what I did? Lord, he must regret the day he ever gave me that job after the scene I caused.' Colour stained her cheeks a brilliant carmine as she remembered the little fiasco in the restaurant.

'Mmm, do you know I'd almost forgotten about that. Shows what an effect you have on me, young lady, but I shall keep it in mind and work out a suitable punishment later! However, that wasn't why he rang.'

'It wasn't?'

The wicked gleam in his blue eyes was playing havoc with her brain again, making it difficult to frame even the simplest of thoughts. She frowned as she tried to concentrate, then gasped. 'It's not Chrissie, is it? She's all right, isn't she, Aaron?'

'She's fine, but Jack sounds a bit worse for wear. Shock, I'd say.'

'Shock? Aaron! What are you talking about? Why should Jack be shocked?'

'It's not every day that one becomes the father of twins, is it? I should think that Jack has every reason to feel shocked.'

'Twins! You can't...there must be...but no one mentioned twins!' Stunned by the news, Kate could only stare open-mouthed at Aaron, then she began to laugh until the tears rolled down her cheeks.

'But isn't that just like Chrissie to pull such a stunt? Sheer magic.'

'Mmm, yes. But it does leave you with a bit of a problem, Kate.' He tilted her chin, looking into her eyes with an expression on his face which made her pulse leap.

'What problem?' she just managed to whisper, her eyes lingering on the tantalising curve of his mouth.

'Well, surely it's going to be difficult being aunt to not just one but two babies—a boy and a girl, I might add. I think you'll need help to carry out your responsibilities properly.'

'Will I? You could be right, so what do you suggest?'

Inching up on her tiptoes, Kate brought her mouth closer to his, shuddering as she felt the warmth of his breath cloud on her skin.

'That you marry me and provide those poor children with an uncle.'

'Marry you! Oh, Aaron!' The words escaped from her lips just an instant before he dipped his head and kissed her until she was breathless.

'Was that a yes or a no?' he asked when he finally drew back, smiling lovingly at her.

'*Yes* . . . yes and yes again!' she cried joyfully, then swiftly pulled his mouth down to hers once more.

Have You Ever Wondered If You Could Write A Harlequin Novel?

Here's great news—Harlequin is offering a series of cassette tapes to help you do just that. Written by Harlequin editors, these tapes give practical advice on how to make your characters—and your story—come alive. There's a tape for each contemporary romance series Harlequin publishes.

Mail order only

All sales final

- ✂ -

Clip this coupon and return to:

HARLEQUIN READER SERVICE
Audiocassette Tape Offer
3010 Walden Ave.
P.O. Box 1396
Buffalo, NY 14269-1396

I enclose my check/money order payable to HARLEQUIN READER SERVICE for $5.70 ($4.95 + 75¢ for delivery) for EACH tape ordered. My total check is for $ _____ .
Please send me:

☐ Romance and Presents   ☐ Intrigue
☐ American Romance   ☐ Temptation
☐ Superromance   ☐ All five tapes ($21.95 total)

Name: _____

Address: _____ Apt: _____

City: _____ State: _____ Zip: _____

NY residents add appropriate sales tax.   AUDIO-H1D

HARLEQUIN

Romance®